HOPELESSLY DEVOTED

SCORNED WOMEN'S SOCIETY BOOK #3.5

PIPER SHELDON

WWW.SMARTYPANTSROMANCE.COM

COPYRIGHT

Print Edition
ISBN: 978-1-949202-81-6

DEDICATION

To J.R., always

And to you reading this ... Yes, you!

CHAPTER 1

WILLIAM

The man in my bed was beautiful. I stood at the threshold of the bathroom to admire the view of the stranger. The outside streetlight cast through the window to highlight his sleeping form. Sprawled as he was, the sheet covered just half of one leg exposing one perfectly shaped calf. The toned muscles of his back narrowed down like an arrow that seemed to point right to his phenomenal ass. In the low light of the night his shaggy dark blond hair was almost enough to make me think ... if I just squinted just right ...

"Admiring the view?" He rolled over and the illusion was broken by the American accent and brown eyes.

"Yes." I smiled as best as I could for being unable to feel how the left side of my mouth lifted. It gave the impression of a coy smirk. Or so I've been told.

"Why don't you come back to bed?" He lifted the sheet to give me more of a show. Well, he had the same cockiness at least.

I ran a hand over my beard and contemplated the offer briefly. I was tempted. I couldn't remember his name. We met at a bar. I was drunk enough. He was close enough. I took him home, taking advantage of having the apartment to myself. I hadn't meant to fall asleep after we fooled around but now I wanted him to leave me alone to be with my thoughts.

My phone vibrated on the bedside table. He was closer and reached for it. He handed it over but not before his gaze flitted across the picture on the screen unapologetically.

"Sanders? Cutie."

I frowned.

"Sorry. I didn't mean to look," he teased with flirtation in his gaze. "Only one reason a man calls this time of night."

"He's my partner."

The man raised a well-manicured eyebrow and pursed his lips before saying, "He can join us."

"Business partner," I clarified gruffly.

"Too bad," he said with a flirtatious pout.

"I have to answer it." I hated how my voice sounded, hated that I had to talk at all. It was better when there was no talking.

He just shrugged and reached for his own phone.

I cleared my throat and gave a pointed look to his jeans lying across the floor.

He stood unabashedly and sighed. "I'll just be going, then."

I turned away to answer.

"Hello?" I whispered.

"Skip. Skippo. My man," Sanders said.

"What time is it?" I asked even though I knew it was after midnight. I didn't want him to know I was awake. I didn't want him to know somebody was here.

"I messed up." Sanders' voice was high and manic. I knew this voice. There was a long call ahead. I muted the line and said, "I'll walk you out," to the man watching me.

"No need. I'm a big boy," he said. He kissed my cheek and started to walk away. Right before I unmuted the phone, he turned back and said, "Hope your friend knows how you feel about him."

I ground my teeth but couldn't find the words to defend our friendship. Many people have accused me of that over the years. But Sanders only saw me as a brother. And that was fine. We were lucky to have such a strong relationship. I was lucky.

He shrugged and I unmuted myself. "Okay. Hold on. Waking up. Just give me a second."

I lied because it was easier this way. We didn't talk about my hookups not because he cared, because I cared.

"You messed up? You've been gone barely one day," I said.

"Yup."

The cute man gave one last flirty wave before leaving. Not for the first I wondered if I would have given him a chance, would it have led to something more? There was an attraction at the bar that seemed to be gone now. Plus, I didn't have time for a relationship right now. Not when Sanders needed me. He just lost his father and was not doing well.

"Okay. Back up." I went to the kitchen and turned on the kettle. "Start from the beginning."

Sanders was obsessing. He shared everything from when he left Denver for Green Valley, Tennessee. He told me it was to help our struggling corporate adventure company, Outside the Box, but I knew it was because of the woman he met, Roxy. The regret was clear in his voice. Things weren't going like he hoped they would. He thought he'd show up to Green Valley and confess his feelings and everything would be better.

That did not happen. She freaked out.

I warned him to give her some space. I had actually met Roxy once. She was like me in a lot of ways and I imagined Sanders showing up to confess his love … Okay, well, that analogy didn't work. But I knew she wouldn't like it. She would need time to process and he needed to understand that.

Sanders felt guilty about what happened at the conference but he was making up for it by finding a new obsession. I didn't like how he sounded. I didn't like how close this all happened to the death of his father. I sighed to myself.

"You know, I was planning on going out there anyway. I'd been looking at flights," I said. I reached for my laptop.

"What? No, mate, you know I'm fine," he said with his fake laugh.

"You're sure?" He could fool others but he never could fool me.

3

"Of course. I always am. I'll clear this up. And I will nail this account. Getting more business by the day. All good things."

I closed my eyes again, rubbing them until I saw spots.

"It'll be fine," he said and I could hear the sleep in his voice finally settling in.

He needed me. He needed me to talk him off ledges and advise him on what to do. I was here to take care of him.

"Okay, Sanders. Just be careful," I said softly.

"Hmm," he hummed already drifting off. I disconnected the call to let him sleep.

I needed to go to him and make sure he was okay. It was my job to make sure he was okay. This was how things worked. Ever since he saved my life, I've been saving his. He was there for me when nobody else was. He came off as so strong but he was more sensitive than most. I had to protect him.

Looked like I was going to Tennessee.

CHAPTER 2

WILLIAM

*T*he drag queen blew me a kiss and I pretended to catch it and press it to my heart. My unintentional smirk got me a wink in return. Three drinks in and the tension had started to melt away. Coming to Knoxville was the right decision. The best-reviewed gay bar was having a drag show and these queens were just the over-the-top distraction that I didn't know I needed.

Each lady was more over the top than the last and I was happy to get lost in the warmth of the atmosphere and loud music. I sat in a small booth in a dark corner by myself. I wasn't looking to meet anybody tonight, but if I saw somebody that seemed interested, I didn't know if I had the strength to say no. My first day in Green Valley had taken so much out of me.

Nobody seemed to pay attention to me. Better that way. I wasn't great company tonight. Or ever. That wasn't ever an issue when most of the time I met guys in the bar or gym. There was never a lot of talking.

The theme tonight was "Ladies of Broadway" and the fiercest green queen dressed as Elphaba just lip-synched her heart out to a recording of "Defying Gravity." The whole bar cracked up at the innuendo of her hip thrusts and exactly what defied gravity.

She finished her number with a very pointed, "And you can't bring me down," as she dropped to her knees. Applause filled the bar.

Even in the happy atmosphere, an image of Sanders came unbidden at the poignant lyrics. The true lyrics. He always thought he could fly without limits. He always pushed himself too high. He was Icarus, and I chased under him with arms wide open. Sanders' fall today shook me more than I could let on. Things were moving too fast. Even for him. I couldn't shake this impending sense of doom. I felt disconnected from my body and on edge. I needed to get out of my head for a little while. I needed to ground myself in my body and forget about the way Sanders looks at Roxy. Or how it felt like something was irrevocably changing in my life.

I swallowed down the rest of my Jameson when I thought of his pale face under the icy clear water of the rushing stream. I squeezed my eyes tight to push the image away. It was replaced with the image of their longing gazes on the Lodge couch today. Sanders was worse off than I thought. He was already acting reckless. This thing with Roxy was more than a harmless crush. I scrubbed my hand over my beard and shook clear the images of them. The room spun as I blinked back to focus on the show around me. I needed to drink some water. I hadn't eaten enough for this level of drinking.

A loud voice from the speakers broke through the haze. "Next up, our very own hussie from Down Under will take a break to sing. You heard that right, ladies, no recording for this bitch. Those are all her own pipes. Please welcome Sandra NoDee to the stage."

As the emcee stopped talking, the flashing colored lights stripped down to one spotlight on the small stage. The music was a mashup of sound clips and songs from the movie *Grease* like, "Look at me, I'm Sandra Dee," and something about virginity. Also mixed in with, "Howya doin', hot stuff?"

On stage was the Sandy Dee of the end of the film. This queen had blonde hair teased to the sky and leather pants that revealed just how good she could tuck. The bar whooped and hollered as she turned around to shake her ass in her tight pants. Her Adam's apple was prominent through all the makeup and her calves threatened to break through the seams of the leather, but she wore the hell out of the outfit and she knew it. She strutted around the stage, snapping fake gum and patting her skyscraper blonde hair.

I laughed with the rest of them. She shouted, "Shut up, you shrimps on the barbie. I'm about to sing."

Sanders would have cringed at the painful attempt at an Australian accent. I took another deep drink. It seemed there was nowhere I could go without being reminded of Sanders on some level.

The steel guitar twanged loudly in the now quiet bar. I finished my drink and whispered to order another when the server came around.

It wasn't the high sweet voice of Olivia Newton-John but lower and equally lovely. She leaned against a barstool, winding the long cord around fingers with inch-long nails.

The whole bar grew rapt in her words. None of us were the first hearts broken, but the pain was universally felt of unrequited love. Her melodic rich tenor rang through the air and the energy shifted to that maudlin sentimentality that only a group of drunk people can evoke. This song hit different when I'd been drinking and feeling sorry for myself.

Couples wrapped their arms around each other, rocking and sharing sad smiles. Some leaned in for a kiss. All around me affection and love. And here I was sad and alone, drinking myself morose, thinking about my straight best friend as a drag queen made me choke up. This was definitely a low point in my life. A sharp pain in my chest felt like somebody was stomping on it with Sandra NoDee's stilettos. The words hit too close to home. There *was* nowhere to hide. I was beyond out of my head, here in a foreign city chasing after a wounded Sanders, only to watch him literally fall over a woman.

A group of women in the corner—dressed for a bachelorette party— fluttered their hands at their faces, tearing up. They clearly interpreted the song in a much happier manner than me. I saw a futile and unrequited love that never stops hurting. They saw the devotion of impending marriage vows. That's what being in a relationship did to a person.

Sandra NoDee stepped off the stage in patent leather stilettos, gracefully making her way through the crowd as money was slipped casually into her hands and outfit. She sang so beautifully people were more than happy to shell out the cash. Though I was hidden in the corner, I could sense the moment she honed in on me. My loneliness flashed like a beacon in the darkness.

She came to stand in front of me, holding out a hand until I grabbed it and stood. She made an over-the-top shocked face and fanned herself when I came to stand almost equal to her height despite those insane heels. She looked me up and down dramatically as the crowd whistled at me. I flushed down at my shoes. I never felt comfortable being in this body, and when I got "good looking," I only felt more self-conscious.

She sang directly to me. She held the word "you" out so perfectly it spread goose bumps down my arms. She spoke to my soul. No matter what, I wouldn't stop being devoted to Sanders. He was the reason for who I am today. This passing fling with Roxy was just that. He'd come crawling back home when he realized what a strong team we were.

The whole room watched us and I felt my emotions crawl up my throat, stealing my words. I hated being the center of attention. After she finished singing, she asked my name and put the microphone to my mouth.

The words wouldn't come. I couldn't make myself speak. My Adam's apple bobbed uselessly in my throat. The whole room waited and I felt every second like a vicious sunburn on the back of my neck. If I tried to speak now, it would come out as a stutter. A couple guys whistled to encourage me. Somewhere the whispers started and the sympathetic awes. My stage fright was painfully obvious.

The light in the room shifted. It was like my brain lifted out of my body and disassociated from me completely. My fingertips began to tingle and my breath came too fast. I'd felt this before. I knew what was coming. Usually Sanders was there to walk me through them. But Sanders wasn't here, was he? Sanders was nowhere to be seen. Sanders was mooning over a woman. Being taking care of by her. Forgetting about me and the life we built together in Denver.

I mumbled some weak apology and pushed past the queen to the exit. Behind me I heard her say, "I'm known to leave men speechless." The crowd cheered and the show went on.

I couldn't breathe. I couldn't stop the panic attack now. It was here. I just needed space. I needed to get away from people.

I was so embarrassed. So ashamed by my weakness. What was wrong with me? I was an idiot. I was such a sad pathetic idiot.

I made my way to an alley that was free of people. I gulped breaths of air but it was too late. It wasn't working. I couldn't catch my breath. What sort of man has a panic attack at a drag show? What would people say? I am a freak. I am all alone. I'm so alone.

CHAPTER 3

JACK

I've worked with enough troubled kids to recognize the signs of someone trying to lose themselves. I had my eye on the hot lumberjack since the moment he walked in. Me and a few others kept shooting him glances in a futile attempt to get his attention but he was in a whole other world tonight. All my warning bells warned me, "This one has issues. Stay Away!"

I'd let the others take their shot with the hot mess express. And damn, he was hot. He had this intense gaze that even a lighthearted drag show couldn't shake. His strong bearded jaw worked with each swallow of his drink, so it was nearly impossible to look away. Though it was hard to get a good look at his build, his broad shoulders nicely filled out his flannel shirt.

Okay, so I would look, but I wouldn't touch. Instead, I chatted with some guys I saw here often. There were locals of Knoxville and one was a member on the UT staff with me. I only glanced to the sexy lumberjack once or twice. I wouldn't let myself be drawn to him. I wasn't in the market of saving anyone from their demons. Been there, done that.

I managed to ignore him decently well too until Sandra NoDee made him stand up during her stunning rendition of "Hopelessly Devoted." The whole bar had a similar reaction to me. Shock and awe. He was a gorgeous hunk of mountain man. His bearded jaw was sharp, his cheeks were chiseled like he'd been handcrafted out of a wet dream. His longish brown hair was slicked back in messy waves, causing one strand to come loose over his forehead when he blushed at the ground. His cheeks and neck were splotched with red with all the attention on him. He tried to smile but only half of his mouth lifted in the attempt. I couldn't help but laugh and shake my head. This poor guy was so out of his element. Why else had he hidden himself in the shadows, hoping to be avoided? Being made the center of attention by the literal center of attention was probably his worst nightmare. What a curse for someone that good looking to be shy.

No. This wasn't just shy. I watched him closely, really watched him. His breaths were coming faster. He flexed his fists repeatedly like he was trying to get the blood flowing back to his fingers. He looked like he was seconds away from a freak-out.

On cue, he shoved his way past the queen.

"Don't do it," I told myself, turning back to the bar. "Not your problem."

But the poor guy … Everybody needed a helping hand from time to time.

"Shit." I sighed, slamming the rest of my beer. I threw down some cash and jogged to the exit.

He was nowhere in sight. I rounded the corner behind the club into an alley and found him tucked away out of sight behind some scaffolding. He was crouched, back to the wall of the building as bass thumped distantly through the thick brick. His head was in his hands, messy hair sticking up between his fingers. His shoulders were up as he curled in on himself, like a kid preparing to be kicked.

"Shit," I swore again, seeing such a big man brought down by his own internal demons. The sight broke my heart. I would just make sure he was okay before I left well enough alone.

He was in a full-blown state when I got to him. His breaths were way too shallow. His body convulsed with tremors and sweat had made the hair around his temples damp. I leaned down toward the stranger knowing it was already too late for me to go back. Whatever was happening to this man, it's clear he was in a bad state. Humans needed to help each other. If we couldn't do that, then what is even the point?

"Hey, man. Are you okay?" I asked in a soothing tone.

His only response was to flinch and curl even more in on himself.

I lowered into an uncomfortable squat in front of him, careful not to touch anything. Thank you, Suzie Samuels, for my newfound flexibility because there wasn't a clean surface to be found. I balanced awkwardly on the balls of my feet.

"What's going on?" I asked again, louder this time.

I lowered my face to try and get his attention. His head lifted and he seemed surprised to find he wasn't alone. His gaze was unfocused and his worried eyes wouldn't stay still. His dark eyebrows were contorted in a pitiful grimace.

"I-I don't know," he gasped out between shallow intakes of breath.

His color was greenish and sure enough sweat dotted his brow as he gasped for air.

"My name is Jack Jones. I'm Red Cross certified and I'm going to see if I can help you, okay?"

The man only nodded his head.

"Can you tell me your name?" I asked, hoping to distract him.

His hands dropped to wrap around his stomach as he rocked slightly. "I-I can't breathe."

"You're breathing right now," I said. "You're going to be okay. I'm going to check your pulse. Is it okay if I touch you?"

I waited for him to nod permission before gently pressing two fingers to the pulse point at his neck. His heartbeat raced out of control.

"Anything else wrong?" I asked.

"Feel weird. Tingling. I think I'm dying."

"Yeah. I bet it feels that way. You seem to be having a panic attack. They are a real mind fuck," I explained.

His head nodded and then shook no before his face crumpled. "I'm sorry. This is so embarrassing."

"Hey, man, nothing to be sorry about. These things happen. You aren't doing anything wrong."

He swallowed, his eyes squeezed shut tight.

"Let's try and hijack that brain of yours. It's trying to help you but it's sending the wrong signals. If I ask you to take a deep breath, do you think you could try and do that for me?"

His head shook furiously. "Can't breathe."

"You're breathing right now. It feels like you can't, but if you're talking, you *are* breathing. It's all good." I reassured him but wasn't sure that the words were getting through. "Okay? You are breathing." I grabbed his hand and placed it on his own chest. "Feel that? That's you taking air in and out, my friend."

This time he took a deeper but shuddering breath.

"I'm right here. I won't leave you alone. You're not alone. You're going to be okay." The words from my training came naturally. My concern for him was real.

He sucked in his lips over and over, chewing on them as his chest hiccuped. His eyes welled with tears, but I instinctually understood that if he broke down, it would only add to his humiliation and make his attack worse.

"Have you ever had a panic attack before?" I asked.

He nodded.

"Okay. So you know that you're going to get through it. You've gotten through it all before. No worries."

"I'm d-dying." His shoulders were bunched up to his ears.

"No way. I won't let that happen."

He looked up at me and it's like he saw me for the first time, really saw me. I smiled the left side of my face, popping the left dimple. It was my best dimple.

"I'm so embarrassed," he repeated.

"No reason to be embarrassed. I've been here. It's the worst. Our brains are evil bastards."

He huffed a short laugh and I felt a small victory.

"Tell me your name. Let's start there," I said.

"S-s-s."

"It's okay. No rush. Whenever you're ready."

I reached out to squeeze his knees without thinking. His gaze shot to me and I worried I'd just made everything worse.

He took a deep stuttering breath.

"William," he managed but his breaths were still coming faster than I would have liked.

"William. Nice to meet you. As I said, I'm Jack."

He still hadn't brushed off my touch. With panic attacks, it could go either way. Some people needed space and to be alone like a wounded animal. Others appreciated the company, and to not feel alone. I ventured another guess and squeezed gently. He sighed.

"William, I'm right here. And the good news is, you're almost through this. Soon you're gonna be able to take more deep breaths, okay?"

"So embarrassed," he repeated and I could tell it took all his strength not to give in and cry. This guy broke my fucking heart. I wanted to tell him to just let it all out, give in to the pain, but my gut told me that would cause him to shirk back into himself.

"So that singer was pretty good, huh?" I said and his face immediately contorted. Definitely not the right route to take. Of course. That's what caused his freak-out. *Way to go, Jones.*

The mistake caused my own energy to shake. I was stronger than this. I was great in a crisis but this guy was hitting me different. I wobbled as I lost balance, still trying to avoid touching the ground at all costs. As I toppled, his arms shot out to grab me before I fell ass backwards on the ground. He gripped my upper arms and I still gripped his thighs.

"Thanks." I swallowed.

His breaths came easier now though, the distraction helped.

"Well, now I'm a little embarrassed." I give him my best grin. "Pretend I smoothly transitioned into sitting. In fact, when you play this memory back, pretend I'm the sexiest man you've ever seen and I gallantly saved the day instead of falling and making things worse."

He chuckled softly as he released me. And a little color finally rose to his cheeks. He took a deep breath in before letting out a long audible breath. His head dropped back against the wall, eyes closed.

"Feel a little better? Those fuckers are the worst," I asked.

He nodded with his eyes still closed making a soft sound of agreement. It probably wasn't cool to check out a man who was struggling but the strong column of his neck was distracting. The thick muscles and tendons flexed as his Adam's apple rose and fell with a swallow. It was hard not to imagine his head thrown back with a groan of satisfaction.

He relaxed further so that his legs kicked out to the side. I sat cross-legged in between him, hands still rubbing without thought.

William brought his hands to clasp on top of his head, accentuating thick arms that pulled his plaid shirt tight. I looked away only to find that his shirt had ridden up to reveal a spattering of dark curls across a tight abdomen.

I was all too aware of the heat growing inside me. This guy was dealing with shit that I didn't need to be getting mixed up with but my body, as always, missed the memo. This attraction needed to be shut down.

When I looked up, he watched me with hooded eyes. His gaze flicked to my hands and I pulled them back from his muscular thighs back to my own.

"Thanks." His voice was so soft it was hardly audible. "I don't—I'm not usually."

"No worries, man. I'm trained for stuff like this. I'm just glad I spotted you."

He moved to stand. I popped up first—not easy for a lengthy guy—to hold out a hand to help him. "Take your time," I advised.

He slowed his movements. One hand scooted up the wall to help him balance. Standing, we were almost matched in height, which says a lot. He out-bulked me by a few dozen pounds.

"That okay?" I discovered my hands were on him again, this time his shoulders with the pretense of helping him balance.

He nodded again. Short on words this one. He said more during his panic attack than since.

He flicked a glance to where I held him and I dropped my arms back to my side. The tension had shifted and I worried I'd read this guy all wrong. He ran a hand over his neck, looking down the alley back toward the bar. I wondered if he felt awkward now that I'd seen him in such a state. Was he ready to prove he's a man's man? Or rather a manly man.

"I don't remember coming out here," he said.

I relaxed out of a fighting stance I hadn't known I'd taken.

"I saw you rush out and could tell something was wrong."

"Thank you." He studied me in stolen glances. "I still can't believe I did that." His words slurred gently as he spoke. At first I thought it was from drinking but there was a long scar hidden under his thick beard, hardly noticeable unless you stared very closely. And apparently I was. It tugged his lip down lightly when he spoke, creating a soft speech impediment.

"No worries," I said.

He ran a hand over his chin when I was caught staring. He straightened his shoulders, adding formality between us that wasn't there before.

"Uh, thank you. For not leaving me," he said.

I shook my head, suddenly short on words.

I didn't want to get mixed up with this guy and yet I didn't know that I could let him go just yet.

"Do you live around here?" As soon as I said it, I regretted it. It was like come-on 101. "I just mean, you probably shouldn't be driving just yet," I quickly added.

"Rideshare. I'm staying over in Green Valley."

My eyebrows shot up in surprise. "Want me to give you a lift? I have a friend that lives over there, it's not far."

"No," he said shortly. "Thanks but no. I've ruined your night enough."

"You haven't ruined anything." I smiled at him openly, hoping to bring back a little bit of that closeness I sensed earlier.

His gaze moved over my face. He was so hard to read hidden behind that scruffy beard, intense stare, and messy hair.

Tell me you don't want me to go yet. I wouldn't make the first move. Not with a man clearly dealing with something.

I shuffled my feet. He started to say something but I broke the awkward silence first. "Are you talking to anybody about these attacks?"

His gaze shuttered. "No. I just—it was a rough day. My friend got hurt."

I stepped closer, again reaching for him, unable to keep my hands to myself. "Is he okay?"

William lifted his eyes to mine, his gaze had this naturally squinted strain to it, like he was always blinking against the midday sun. He shrugged.

"I'm sorry," I said. And I looked to my hand still on his shoulder. He followed my gaze. The air grew thick with unspoken questions.

His nostrils flared and a new something burned behind those mysterious eyes. I should step back now. I needed to put some distance between this guy who only spelled trouble.

And yet I didn't move. I couldn't.

Instead, he did.

Without any warning his hand grabbed the back of my head, pulling me closer until our bodies had almost no space between us. My face hovered just in front of his, searching his dark eyes. He hesitated only to confirm I wouldn't shove him away. I licked my lips and it was the only invitation he needed.

18

CHAPTER 4

WILLIAM

*M*y mouth was on his. He opened to me immediately. Our tongues clashed with intensity that made my heart race harder than it had only a minute ago. If I could have, I might have gasped at the instant pleasure and relief I felt with his lips on mine. Our mouths acted desperate for the other, like we'd known each other forever and not just a few moments.

Any hope I had of maintaining composure was quickly diminishing. He'd already seen me at my worst. Maybe I could show him a bit of my better side. He looped his free arm behind me, closing any space between us. I gripped his hips, thrusting my hardness back into his.

He groaned as I nibbled his bottom lip.

Our kiss shouldn't have felt so good. Lust burned through me in ways I haven't felt in ages. With all the one-night stands, I was turned on, but it wasn't like this. I got through my panic attack only to find this gorgeous man who had helped me. The kiss surprised me as much as it must have surprised him.

I flipped us so that he was now against the wall. I pulled back to look at him.

His deep dimples were emphasized by his surprised grin. He was painted in shades of brown, from his smooth skin, to his beard trimmed short as his hair, to his mischievous eyes that watched me closely. He was my height, maybe a little taller, and his tight white tee emphasized a lean but strong frame. And fuck his lips were so kissable. But it wasn't just how achingly sexy he was. He was here. He sought me out when he saw I was in trouble. He stayed with me at my worst moment.

As I took in every lovely feature of his face, he watched me with a hesitant smile. The side of my mouth lifted subtly. His dimples deepened even more somehow. Fuck, they were adorable. I brought my hands to his cheeks and pulled him back to me, running my thumbs over the indents until they smoothed away into the heady seriousness of our kiss. I kissed him slower this time, more tenderness, a thank-you for helping me through a dark moment. I would be embarrassed. Later I would replay the attack and feel shame, but now I lost myself to this moment.

"Jack," I tested his name on my tongue in a quick break for breath.

The man I would never see again felt like a savior. So different than all the men I'd taken home to numb the pain. I wanted him more than any of them. I ignored how that worried me deep down.

I'd never see him again, let myself have this moment. I needed him now. I needed to take this shot while I could. Let me be the selfish one for once.

I was eager and desperate for him. It felt like a fever. I dropped my hands to grab his ass and thrust myself against him. He was as rock hard as I was, as I massaged him there. His ass was phenomenal. It inflamed me. I kissed him so hard I tasted blood.

He broke the kiss stepping back, holding up a hand. "Hold up. Slow down." He ran a hand over his mouth, looking at me with disheveled confusion.

I reached forward and pulled him back to me. I kissed up the column of his neck. "I don't want to," I mumbled against his hot skin.

He groaned and his hips rocked against me. "Fuck," he moaned out. His hands moved to tug through my hair.

I so badly wanted him in my mouth. I moved without thinking. His hands in my hair remained, frozen with indecision. Not stopping, not guiding either. I was on my knees in the dirty alley and didn't give a fuck.

The recklessness of this decision made me feel high. I wanted him to use my mouth and I didn't care about anything else.

"No. Wait." He pushed my shoulders until I looked up at him.

I held his gaze as I ran my hand over his rock-hard dick.

"Jesus," he swore. "You're fucking gorgeous."

This time I didn't blush or turn away. I just squeezed him through the jeans he strained against.

He groaned out in frustration. "No, William. Not here. Come on." He pulled me to stand. I allowed him to pull me up but that didn't stop me from going back to his neck to lick and suck. I fondled the button of his jeans. I had to feel the length of him against my palm. It practically itched with the need.

I felt the buzz from the earlier drinks. I felt the post-panic-attack rush of adrenaline. I felt my lust for him burning me up from the inside out. All of it. I was completely out of control and it felt so nice to be so out of my head.

"Stop." His voice was firm enough to cut through the haze. I dropped my hand and lowered my forehead to his shoulder, panting. "Just stop, man."

Shame crept back into my senses.

"I'm not strong enough to be the bigger person here," he said with a huff of a laugh.

I buried my face deeper into his neck, not ready to see him. Not ready to feel the pity of his gaze.

"William," he spoke softly. "You're going through something. What kind of man would I be to take advantage of that?"

I sighed, feeling a little triumph as he shuttered with my caressing breath. He groaned and threw his head back.

"Doing the right thing can really suck sometimes." His voice was soft and strained. He moved his hands to my shoulders, thumbs rubbing as they had coaxed me through my panic attack. He gently pushed me back a step.

We held each other's gaze for a long moment. Deep down I knew he was right. I wouldn't be happy with myself later.

"But maybe ..." He cleared his throat and started again. "If you gave me your number, I could take you out sometime."

It was a bucket of ice water to my senses. "No," I said instantly.

His easy smile melted away. A crease appeared between his eyebrows.

"I live in Denver," I added to soften my harshness. He lifted an arm and scratched the back of his neck. "Well, how long will you be in Green Valley?" His voice was cautious with hope.

"Not long." If I could help it.

Jack crossed his arms. "Gotcha."

I wanted him badly. But he was right. I was in no state to get into anything. He deserved more than that. He was *decent.* He helped me when he didn't have to.

Words warred in my brain. I should say something to assure him that the attraction was real, just the timing wasn't right. I'm not right. If I tried now, my words would get tangled on the way out, even if I spoke slowly and enunciated the best I could. I saw him notice my scar earlier. I didn't want to drag any more attention to it. I think I humiliated myself enough for one night.

I waited too long; he broke the silence first. "And you're sure you're okay to get home?"

His kindness only made my frustration worse. I nodded, stuffing my hands into my pockets. I was a real piece of shit.

"Well, good luck to you, William. I hope your friend is okay," he said. He turned away and I watched until he was back around the corner.

I sighed back against the wall, jaw clenching painfully.

Only later would I realize that I hadn't thought of Sanders once since he touched me. I wasn't sure what that meant.

* * *

"You William?" a voice asked from the street.

My phone was still in my hand where I stood at the end of the alley. I hadn't even opened the rideshare app yet. I'd been staring into space for who knew how long. I debated going back after Jack—a feeling which took me completely by surprise. Our encounter left me shaken but I had to tell myself it was just because of his kindness when I had been hurting and nothing more. Not the insane attraction to this man I'd only just met. And yet, I kept picturing those quirked eyebrows and friendly dimples. The concerned way he watched me. The incredible heat when ours mouth met and the overwhelming desire to bring him pleasure, to taste him, to feel his hard …

"Yo, earth to William?" the voice called out.

I blinked at the stranger and stepped closer. In the light of the overhead lamp, I could see it was a gorgeous redhead with expertly shaped eyebrows raised expectantly. She looked me up and down before popping her bubble with a loud snap. "You must be him. Jack said you were a looker."

I frowned at the ground. Even after I was an asshole to him, he continued to look out for me.

"I just dropped my last ride. I'm heading back toward Green Valley. Speak now or forever hold your peace," she said.

I stepped toward the car, my chin still tucked as I looked up at her with hesitation.

"Woo, he was not kidding. You really have that smolder down, doncha?"

"I—"

"If it makes you more comfortable, I could give you Jack's number if you want." She smiled in a way that told me that's exactly what she'd hoped I do. "You know, call to verify I'm not a psycho." She looked up and around, then added, "Or at least that I won't hurt you."

"I'll take my chances," I said and got in the car.

"I'm Gretchen LaRoe, pleased to meet ya." I shook her extended hand. Her grip was as confident as her personality. "Where ya headed?" She snapped her gum loudly enough to make me flinch.

"Donner Lodge."

"Ah yes. Making lots of trips there these days," she said with not a pinch of salt to her tone.

She checked her mirrors before pulling out into traffic without another word. Her hands gripped the steering wheel as she continued to chomp on her gum. The incessant snapping and popping grated my already frayed nerves. I took some deep breaths to control my neurosis. This stranger had gone out of her way to help me. She was friends with Jack. I needed to chill.

"You doing okay?" She threw me a concerned look before merging on the interstate that would take us back to Green Valley.

How much had Jack shared about our encounter? He hadn't struck me as the type to gossip, but I felt her watching me as though I might crumble any second.

"Fine," I said.

"Ah. You're one of those strong and silent types. You should know that only makes me talk more." She snapped her gum loudly again.

This time I couldn't fight the sigh that came out of my flared nostrils.

"You sort of remind me of my best friend." She cut herself off with a frown. "Not that we're talking at the moment. We had a fight. I mean, I guess. I was just trying to help her get with this guy she was crushing on and she full-on freaked out for no reason. So she hadn't expected to see him again." She chatted on and I counted the seconds until I was back at the Lodge. I was starting to think that I would have rather waited for the rideshare.

"But like, here's the thing, I know her. She's too chicken to go after what she wants without a little shove in the right direction. I know that sounds harsh but I've known her most my life. I know her better than I know myself. She had a moment with this dude but wouldn't let herself give in to it."

It was as if she was talking about me without meaning to.

"People change," I grumbled. I couldn't help myself. She could only see her side of things, and sure, I didn't know the story but there was always more than one side to every story.

"That's true," she said, and to my utter shock she seemed to mull over my words.

I regretted snapping at her. She at least seemed to be listening.

"I mean, I guess I do tend to poke my nose in other people's business. I can't help it. I only want to make the people I care about happy." Her voice was so soft, by the time she finished, it was like a different person spoke. A far cry from the boisterous caricature of a person who first arrived.

"People have to make their own mistakes," I said slowly and carefully so my words didn't get tangled. I had already been rude to her.

"Man, you really do remind me of her." She sighed, and despite my fog of self-pity, I felt for her. She missed her friend. I'd be lost if Sanders and I weren't talking. Was I any better? Every action I took was with him in mind, thinking five steps ahead to keep him safe. People didn't see through his facade of gregariousness to the pain and fear that lingered just under his surface.

"You guys will work it out," I offered lamely.

"Yeah." She went quiet a few more minutes.

The passing forest, so different than Denver, was green and dense even in the dark. The headlights illuminated only what was right in front of the sedan.

When she spoke again her peppy disposition was back. "So how do you know Jack?"

I really didn't want to talk but thought the silence might drive her insane, so I said, "I don't. I uh, just met him tonight." My words started to get tangled at the thought of him, so I stopped talking.

"He's such a good guy. Best friend of one of my gal Suzie's fiancé. He volunteers to help kids. He's a professor of mathematics at UT. He's a real looker too, isn't he?"

She flicked another glance at me. "This is you not getting involved?" I softened my jab with a half grin.

She laughed. "Ah, shit. You're right. Sorry. Sorry. Okay, last thing I'm gonna say, he's just such a wonderful person. He deserves a little fun."

This time I didn't know what to say. Or rather I didn't have anything to say. He was a good guy. That much was obvious from our brief interaction. My head was beginning to throb from grinding my molars. I wasn't the good-time guy Jack deserved. I was a storm cloud of frustration that was heading back to Denver as soon as I got Sanders out of this current predicament.

Best to let this one go. Any minute now my body would forget the taste of him.

CHAPTER 5

WILLIAM

*T*wo days later and I made another mistake. I shouldn't have gone to this bar, Genie's, with Sanders. He made it sound like we were going to meet other people and I thought it would be nice to have some time with him. I hadn't been able to keep a close eye on him with all the time he'd been spending with Roxy.

The moment I walked in, I saw her standing there, waiting for Sanders. Her smile was so genuine when she spotted him. When she saw me, the truth became clear. This was a date and I was the most obvious third wheel.

As soon as Sanders went to the bar, I leaned toward Roxy and asked, "Are you okay?"

She nodded her head, her normally cool features forced a smile. "Of course."

"If I'm intruding …"

"Not at all." She fixed her bangs and sucked in her lips. "I'm glad to see you," she said, and I believed her.

"Me too," I said. I glanced to make sure that Sanders wasn't coming back. "Listen. Sanders brought me because he made it sound like a group thing." My tongue was sluggish in my mouth.

"News to me," she said tightly.

I shouldn't be here and I felt as embarrassed as she must. Sanders, once again, hadn't thought about how his actions might make others feel. I had to explain. He wasn't a bad guy, he just didn't always think things through. He was clumsy with his optimism. She needed to know that he would never internally hurt anybody, let alone somebody he obviously cared so much for. "I think he's just afraid to be alone with you. He knows you want to set boundaries and he's still so raw from his dad's death, I think he's just trying to do the right thing," I over-explained.

Nobody understood Sanders like I did. They thought he was this gregarious force of nature. And he was, to some extent, but he also hid a lot of pain. He pushed it down and acted reckless to feel something other than the fear of losing people that haunted him. Sanders hadn't talked about his father's death at all since it happened. He was in a weird state of denial, moving from one project to the next to occupy his brain.

Roxy's color drained as quick as it came. "His dad's death?"

Shit. "I thought you knew."

"I did but I thought it was years ago."

"No. It was about three weeks ago."

She gasped. "What?"

"He's still—" I stopped talking abruptly and sat back as Sanders walked up.

"They'll come by to get our order." Sanders grinned happily, obliviously, looking between the two of us.

The two lovebirds started talking and I shifted and looked around the country bar. It was pretty packed but I couldn't have felt more alone. My tongue felt dry and heavy in my mouth. This was such a mistake. I shouldn't have come tonight. I shouldn't have come to Green Valley. The way Sanders watched Roxy like a lovesick puppy was a side of him I'd never seen. Hyper-fixation, sure. But this was something new. My stomach churned. I couldn't have felt more uncomfortable.

And then something shifted. An energy I couldn't explain in any sort of tangible way, like that buzz in the air before a thunderstorm. It was as though the universe heard my wallowing and said, *challenge accepted.*

Jack. I felt him before I saw him. It would sound corny if it wasn't true.

A couple approached the table with Jack in tow. Roxy talked to them but I couldn't hear anything for the blood rushing in my ears.

Jack was *here*.

He wore a white dress shirt, the top button open to reveal just a hint of his lean, muscular collarbones. I had run my hands over that body. I had felt the strength that was hidden under his business clothes. His dark dress pants and shoes were pristine and professional. He must have come straight from teaching his summer classes. Not that I checked his class roster after learning where he taught from Gretchen. How could any of his grad students focus if this was what they got to see every week? A twist of jealousy usually reserved for the numerous lovers of Sanders, caught me off guard. I braved myself to look at his face. My fists balled under the table. He looked right at me. His sexy dark eyebrows twisted in confusion while his easy smile assumed the best.

I looked away immediately. Like a coward.

To my absolute horror, the new group was joining us, chairs were being added to the table. I couldn't think. I couldn't speak. My ears burned in humiliation. What were the chances? The universe was fucking with me.

A man named Ford, apparently already aquatinted with Sanders, introduced Jack to me. I had only a fraction of a second to decide how I wanted to handle this. It seemed Jack was also leaving it up to me. He held out his hand, his smile never wavering.

"Nice to meet you," I mumbled and shook his hand, dropping my eye contact.

Shame burned through me. I had never expected … I had hoped maybe … but I never thought.

"Nice to meet you too," Jack said easily after only the slightest hesitation. Whatever he thought was happening, he didn't share our meeting to Sanders or the others.

As we all got situated, Roxy's anxiety grew with my own. The air practically hummed with our shared tension. Her drinks increased as did my rage. It made no sense. The more furious I grew with myself, the more I directed it at him. Every single thing he said pushed me closer to some point I didn't understand. Maybe because I had thought of him so much since the night we met. Maybe because it shook me more than I wanted to admit, but to see that it hardly impacted him at all, ultimately cut at me.

He wasn't doing anything wrong, but the more affable and more understanding he was, the worse I felt, the angrier I grew.

Then another recognizable face joined the group. "Hey, y'all."

It was the nosey redhead that drove me home, Gretchen. I assumed she was acquainted with Jack on some level but was this town really that small or did I really just have the world's worst luck?

Again Roxy and I were the only ones who seemed to find this situation miserable. The atmosphere around us was loose and jovial while she and I retreated into our shell of silence. Gretchen and Jack's flirtation only added to my irritation. I felt like a stick in the mud, and whenever I spoke it was only to snap at Jack. I knew I wasn't being fair but I also couldn't stop.

It didn't take long for me to understand that it was Gretchen who had a hand in the reunion of Sanders and Roxy that night at the drive-in movie. It was hard for me to take Roxy's side in all this after that. This was all too much. I wanted to crawl into a hole until it was time to go back to Denver.

I was about ready to call it a night when Sanders went all macho man on some local at the bar for staring at Roxy. I talked him down from attacking like some frat brother when Jack seemed to notice the tension.

"These girls can take care of themselves, trust me," Jack said easily. "Gretchen probably has a weapon hidden under the table even as we speak."

"I wasn't saying that they couldn't," I snapped.

I was studying my hands but felt Jack stiffen. "I know that. I was just saying—"

Suzie came back, her eyes were wide as they shot around the table. "She slipped out while I was"—her gaze flicked to me and Sanders— "using the facilities," she finished.

Sanders shot up out of his chair. I steadied the drinks he almost knocked over.

"That's sort of her thing, isn't it?" Gretchen said. But the same worry tightened the corners of her eyes. It was the same tenderness in her facade that I sensed when she drove me home.

"I'm going after her," Sanders said with determination. "Skippo, give me the rental, hey?" He reached for the keys.

I handed them over and pulled out my wallet. "I'll come with. Just let me close the tab—"

"There's no time. I got this," he said, hopping on the balls of his feet, searching the bar.

I ground my jaw. He couldn't wait another minute? Really?

"I can take him back to the Lodge," Jack offered.

I couldn't refuse. I couldn't speak. This was not happening.

"I don't bite," he added.

My head throbbed from my jaw clenching so tight.

Sanders was gone without another word. The mood had been killed and the others closed their tabs out too.

There was no more delaying the inevitable.

"Ready, *Skip*?" Jack asked with a slight emphasis on my nickname that nobody else would notice.

* * *

Jack

I PRIDED myself on my gut instinct for people. I typically knew how to handle every situation to gain trust and respect. It came with a lifetime of never quite fitting in. But man, I had read William all wrong. Or Skip. Whoever he was. He had made a clear choice when he pretended not to know me at Genie's Bar. I wouldn't out him to his friends but I wasn't about to go offering him another date. I was amiable and friendly all throughout the night and yet he snapped at everything I said, like *I* was the one to blame for this. I would give him a ride home but that was it. I would stop worrying about him once and for all.

My respect once lost was impossible to get back.

And he hurt me. He lied to me. He pretended not to know me. He was rude to me. And all because I pumped the breaks on a hookup when he was drunk and at his lowest point. Well, wasn't I an asshole.

William and I walked out to my car in silence.

Skip, I corrected.

It was going to be hard to reprogram my brain after all the hours I thought about him. I jerked off to him, pretending I let him finish what he started to offer in that alley, calling out that name as I came onto my stomach. That wrong name. I imagined him calling me up, thanks to Gretchen, and meeting up for drinks or lunch. I had spent way too much time projecting some fantasy onto someone who obviously wanted nothing to do with me. I was good enough for a BJ in an alley but not a real name.

I gripped the steering wheel and tilted my head side to side to stretch my neck.

Skip cleared his throat as though trying to get my attention. The keys were in the ignition but I didn't turn over the engine. I wasn't giving him an inch. If he had something to say, he could say it.

That lasted approximately three more seconds but I couldn't keep myself quiet.

"I wasn't about to out you to your friends. If that's what you were worried about. I would never do that." There was a sharp edge to my voice as I glared out the windshield.

"I didn't think ... Sanders knows ... I don't care if—" He stopped and scrubbed his hands through his hair. He groaned. "Fuck."

I couldn't help myself, I turned toward him in the seat as he balled his fists and glared at them.

"S-s-s," he started. His hair stuck up in all directions. I longed to smooth my fingers through it. He took a deep breath and started again, slowly and softly. "William *is* my real name."

His quiet remorse softened my anger already. So much for holding grudges. So he hadn't lied about that, but it didn't excuse his rudeness.

"Your nickname is Skip?"

"I'm sure you could guess why." He huffed a self-deprecating laugh.

It made me frown. I had a theory but it tightened my chest in sympathy. "No idea," I said.

"I had a stutter. My classmates thought it was hilarious."

My jaw dropped. "Your best friend calls you something meant as torment?"

William lifted his chin. "I chose to be called that. Sanders' dad took me in but his name was William. It was just easier. But it was my choice."

He held my gaze in challenge. I knew a little bit about taking back the power of a word from people who weaponized it.

"I understand that," I said not dropping his gaze.

An understanding passed through us. His brusque personality made more sense. He may be shy and soft spoken to begin with but he also has to choose his words carefully.

"Sanders doesn't call me that to be cruel," he explained. "That's all he's ever known me as. But when I meet new people, I give my real name. So." He cleared his throat. "I just didn't want you to think that I was lying."

I nodded without moving to start the car. We still sat in the parking lot of Genie's. A streetlight illuminated us.

"Sorry I was being a dick," he grumbled. "Back in there. It wasn't about you at all."

"I figured," I said flatly. "Typically, when people treat me like shit, it's due to their own issues and nothing I did."

"Aren't you well-adjusted."

I shrugged. "I've just spent a lot of time dealing with shit. I know what I will and won't put up with now."

He quieted. I was still a little salty about him being a dick. But then again, he apologized and Ford was always a grumpy fuck too. I was used to it. I decided to let it go. After all, I know it's not about me at all. And isn't that a bitch?

"So you and Sanders grew up together?" I asked.

William nodded. I had been curious about the nature of their friendship since I met Sanders. William watched his friend closely all night. Something about it felt more than brotherly to me.

"Ford, you met him back there"—I thumbed toward the bar—"we grew up together too."

His face conveyed the surprise most people had when learning this about Ford and me. "I know. But we're basically brothers. Don't let his grumpy demeanor fool you. Suzie has softened him at least."

"She seems nice. Suzie."

"She is," I said.

"And Gretchen?"

"Oh Gretch. She's crazy but I love her."

"And, uh, Roxy?" he asked.

"I don't know her as well but all the SWS women are badasses."

"SWS?"

I laughed with a shake of my head. "Scorned Women's Society. They aren't very secret about it. There's this guy, Jethro Winston, he made his way through a good portion of the female population of Green Valley before he cleaned up his act. Some of his exes got together to form a little club."

William's eyebrows shot up.

"I know. It doesn't seem like it would work but they're super close and protective of one another." William nodded, his gaze to the side as he processed my words. "Roxy is the hardest to read. I will say, I've never seen her with anybody before. And your Sanders seems smitten with her."

The muscles of his jaw tensed as his nostrils flared.

"Are you not a fan?" I felt defensive of Roxy. All the SWS women were good people.

"Roxy? No. I like her a lot actually. We hit it off in Denver. She wasn't even supposed to meet Sanders if not ..." he mumbled off the rest of his thoughts.

"So you're not a fan of the relationship between the two of them?" I asked, my theory grew more support.

I started the car and started the short drive toward the Lodge.

"Sanders has a whole life back in Denver. He's just avoiding things," he said.

Something clicked that I missed until just then. The friend who'd been hurt when he had his panic attack.

Blond hair, Australian accent ... *Hopelessly Devoted.*

All the pieces fully slid into place.

William wasn't being shitty to me because I was there. I wasn't even in the picture. He was pissed because Sanders is mad for Roxy and he couldn't handle it.

"Sanders is the friend that you were worried about," I asked, keeping myself cool as I breached the topic we both seemed to be avoiding: our almost night together.

I couldn't see him on the dark winding road but I felt him nod.

"His dad just died. He's not … handling things well," he explained, once again defending Sanders.

I frowned. "William was like a dad to you too, wasn't he?"

He grunted what sounded like a sort of yes.

My hand that had been on the stick shift moved to his shoulder. His body heat warmed my hand through his tee shirt. The tensed muscle there sent me back to the night we met. To the images that kept repeating in my head. I dropped my hand again.

"I'm sorry," I said.

He swallowed and nodded.

"Sanders seemed okay tonight," I said. Now I was just prodding but I needed more information. I needed to be sure. There was heat between us. I couldn't fight it but I had been played the fool before.

"He's not. He does this. He gets fixated and jumps from obsession to obsession. And I just—"

"What?" I asked sticking my nose in way too far where it didn't belong.

"I follow him wherever he goes," he said.

A sudden weariness seeped into my bones as I pulled into the Lodge roundabout. When I first saw William tonight, it felt like a second chance, but that was quickly shot down. As he opened up to me, my very silly heart got its hopes up again. But no. I have been down this path before. I wouldn't be anybody's second choice and one thing was very clear, whether William knew it or not.

He was in love with Sanders.

CHAPTER 6

JACK

"*P*ull that booty back. Don't overextend. Arms a little wider. Okay, now kick up. There ya go!" An upside-down Suzie clapped excitedly. "Great job!"

The blood rushed to my head but I was elated to finally accomplish the handspring, thanks to Suzie's twisted-grip technique.

I spread my legs out slowly, gripping the bar the way I had been taught and proud that my flexibility has come this far.

"You're leaning too far to my right." Upside-down Ford appeared in front of me.

I gently tucked back down and off the bar. "Nice to see you too, Ford."

He grinned. "I just thought you'd want to know."

I grabbed my towel and dabbed the sweat off my brow. "What would I do without you?" I said flatly.

"I shudder to think." He went to Suzie to peck her cheek and they shared a secret smile that simultaneously made me happy and jealous. I turned away and did my best to not think of William and the hurt that followed. Ford turned back to me. "You gotta minute?" he asked.

"For you, I have three," I said.

"I'll wipe down the mat and pole for ya," Suzie said.

"I brought more of that cleaning spray I created. It's better for skin." I pointed to the bottle on the floor near my bag.

"I need a favor." Ford flicked a glance to Suzie and pulled me to the corner.

"What's up?" I stretched my arms as he shifted foot to foot. He picked at the cuticle of his thumb. I hadn't seen him this nervous since he told me he was going to propose.

"I have my eye on this house for Suzie and me. It's perfect. A beautiful cabin off Bandit Lake. These houses never become available. Never. You can only inherit them. But I did a favor for that Devlin guy and he got me an in."

"Wow, that's awesome."

And so fast. I knew when Suzie and Ford got engaged, our time living together near the UT campus would be coming to an end. Stripped was in Green Valley and Ford worked mostly from home. It didn't make sense for them to commute to Knoxville all the time. Still. I couldn't help but feel a little sad that this chapter of our lives was coming to an end. I had enjoyed living with them.

I pushed away my selfish feelings.

"Thanks. I'm excited," he said but his pallor conveyed more than a little bit of nerves. "I want to surprise her by taking her to see it and stay there a few nights. But the only time they can do it is this week."

"She's gonna love it, man." It was a perfect place for them. I really was happy for them. And only a little bit jealous. "So you need me to help?"

"I was supposed to take some of the teen guys from Triple F camping this week."

"So we are sticking to that, huh?" I interrupted. He'd taken to calling Ford's Fosters Foundation, "Triple F," though to be honest it didn't roll off the tongue for me.

Ford blinked at me before carrying on. "I know it's a big ask but can you get your TA to cover you Wednesday? It's just two nights, but the campsite was already close to backing out when they heard some had been in the JDC. And the guys were really looking forward to it."

The juvenile detention center was like the first major derail for so many kids. Kids that deserved help and another shot, not being thrown into a system that wiped away their identity. After that, their chances of a life of crime greatly increased.

"Of course. You know I will," I said putting him at ease. "No biggie."

"They insisted on two adults," Ford explained. His grumpy face returned as he spoke. "Ethan is eighteen but they want older chaperones. They think they're going to party or vandalize, I don't know. It's ridiculous. They need a chance to prove that they're trustworthy—"

"Ford." I reeled him back in. "Want me to reach out to Gretchen? Though, I don't know that having her around a group of teen boys is a great idea."

"Oh, no." He shook his head. "That's the best part. I think I forgot to say that. I asked Outside the Box to help. Remember Sanders, the nice Australian guy? Well, his friend Skip said that Sanders had a big client but that he, uh Skip, was available to help. Lucky he's in town."

"Lucky us." My flat tone betrayed me.

"What?" he asked.

"Is it too late to offer Gretchen up instead?"

"What's wrong? I admit, I thought he was a little weird to you that night at Genie's. I didn't know if you noticed."

"Yeah, Ford, I noticed. I'm surprised you noticed, King Oblivious."

Ford pushed his glasses up his nose. "He's got you testy." Then his demeanor changed in an instant. His voice lowered to a threatening register and his cheeks grew ruddy under his trimmed beard. "Did he say something to you? Because if he did, I will—"

"Hold your horses, big fella." Suzie came up seeming to sense Ford's sudden mood switch. She ran her hand over his chest and his shoulders relaxed away from his ears. "What's wrong?" Suzie looked to me and Ford.

"Nothing," I said.

At the same time, Ford said, "Skip said something terrible and now we're going to hurt him."

I guffawed. Ford was really leaning into this more protective persona. His hand snaked around Suzie's waist and he pulled her tight. "I won't have any more people I love getting hurt."

"While I appreciate the sentimentality," I said, "it's not like that."

"I wouldn't have expected that from Skip. He seemed so gentle the other night at Genie's. Like a big old grumpy teddy bear." She nuzzled into Ford. "I have a soft spot for those."

Ford frowned as he considered this. Before I could give him any more reasons to hate the guy, I said, "I really don't mind working with him. I just"—I scratched my head—"I had a little crush on him, for a second, but he's hung up on someone else."

I didn't delve into the details of the panic attack and the gay club nor the brief and exquisite make-out session. Fuck, it was magical. But no. I saw the way he looked at Sanders. I'm not an idiot. I'm not going down that road ever again.

"How dare he. Has he met you?" Ford said.

"His loss," Suzie agreed.

I chuckled. "Thanks, guys. But it's not a big deal. I swear. I'm happy to help."

"Only if you're sure?" Ford scrutinized me. He remembered all too well the time my heart was broken. "It's a real sunova bitch that you can't help who you love."

"I don't love him. Shit, I hardly know him," I said all too quickly.

Ford blinked in confusion as Suzie snorted and then explained, "I think he meant Skip. Skip can't help who he loves."

"Oh, right. Yeah." And I did know a little something about that too, didn't I? I shared a look with Ford. He had helped picked up all the pieces after. "I'm sure it'll be fine," I said.

"You're a lifesaver," Ford said. "Better get ready for our trip too." Ford winked obviously at me. Suzie looked at Ford and squinted her eyes suspiciously.

The two left me to collect myself. My palms were inexplicably sweaty. The problem wasn't with me. I had tried to be real. William was the one working through some shit.

It was just a couple of nights in the woods and he would go back to Denver. I would be just fine.

Nothing to worry about at all.

* * *

William

I TUCKED the notecards discreetly in the back pocket of my hiking pants and took a deep steadying breath. The lobby of the Lodge was fairly busy for a Wednesday morning with people checking in. Jack and the bus of teens would be here any minute and Sanders was here to see me off. He'd been so caught up with Roxy this week that I'd hardly seen him at all. This trip was one of the few things making me feel like I had business being out here.

"You got everything?" Sanders asked as I double-checked my camping backpack.

I nodded.

"Of course you do. You probably have a spreadsheet you checked off," he teased.

He was right though. Nerves made my mouth dry and I couldn't share his happy chatting this early morning.

I cleared my throat but couldn't seem to dislodge the pressure there.

Sanders grabbed my shoulders and squeezed until I looked into his light blue eyes. "You're gonna be great. You're prepared. And so damn lovable." He shook me gently.

Heat flushed my cheeks with the warmth of his words. He always knew what I needed to hear. I wanted to say something, it was stuck with that lump in my throat. In another moment Sanders had moved on and dropped his hands.

"Ask them what dapping is too, hey," Sanders said as he poorly attempted to shoot his arms out and tuck his head.

His endless blue eyes danced with mirth. He was trying to soothe my nerves by acting like an idiot. I laughed and shook my head. "Pretty sure it's dabbing and it's no longer cool if you know about it."

He shrugged. "See, you already know more than me."

He bounced on the balls of his feet and his gaze kept flicking around the lobby. He seemed more wound up than normal. His cheeks held a glow that wasn't there previously.

"Are you okay?" I asked.

He grinned ear to ear. "Oh yeah."

"So things are going well?" The effervescent joy bubbling out of him told me his relationship with Roxy had moved past just a friendship.

"Very, very well," he said with a bounce of his eyebrows.

"With the client I mean."

He flicked a glance to me. "Of course, hey. I told you I had this trip in the bag. Everything is working out perfectly."

I tugged the paracord of my pack tighter than necessary. It was fine. Let him get it out of his system. It wouldn't be long until he had to get back to reality.

"When I get back, after MooreTek leaves, we're heading back to Denver, right?" I asked carefully.

His gaze flitted around avoiding me, looking for Roxy. She entered the lobby, looking lovely as always in a black skirt and suit jacket. Her gaze went straight to Sanders. They shared a look and a blush lifted to her cheeks.

So definitely not just friends anymore.

Her eyes flicked to me and she waved with a little smile. I don't think I'd ever seen her smile so big.

"Sanders," I snapped.

He turned reluctantly back to me with a smile so big it had to hurt. "Yup. What's up, Skippo?"

"You're gonna reach out to Dev and the team while I'm gone, right?"

"Of course, of course."

"Sanders, this is important."

"I'm gonna go meet Roxy. The client will be here soon," he said, already walking away.

I glared at my backpack and shoved it up onto my shoulder. My fist balled until my short nails dug into my palms. If he thought that I would just sit around and wait—

"And, Skippo?" His shoes were back in my line of sight. He grabbed my shoulders until I looked at him. There was nowhere to hide when he looked at me like that, deep ocean eyes imploring and head cocked so that a lock of blond hair fell in his eyes. "You're gonna do great. They're all gonna love you." He pulled me into a hug and slapped me on the back. "How could they not?"

I hugged him back briefly. "Thank you," I whispered.

"Love you," he called as he retreated.

"Love you too," I said as I watched him walk away from me and up to Roxy. He stopped a few inches in front of her. I couldn't hear them but their body language remained professional. Save the look passing between them that could melt their clothes off. When she spoke, he watched her with so much focus there was nobody else in the world.

She straightened her fringe and smiled. Again. Bigger than before. Seemed she did that a lot now. Her eyes shone as they looked into his eyes.

Was this different this time for Sanders? Was this more than a passing fling?

I had the overwhelming feeling that I was in one of those moments where I would look back and realize that was the moment everything changed. A deep ache in my chest took me so suddenly I felt my breath being sucked away. My heart began to race.

No. Not here. Not now.

When I first talked to Ford about this camping trip, I'd tried to talk to Sanders about it. He sensed I was on the verge of another attack and talked me down. I had tried to explain why I was so nervous but I couldn't even explain it. I made it seem like it was having to be around teens, he knew I never had the best track record fitting in, but it was more than that. It was the idea of being alone with Jack. I couldn't talk to Sanders about that though, could I? Plus, Sanders had been super distracted and hard to pin down. I wished I could share with him the way he did with me. Now that familiar sinking feeling of an impending attack was returning so soon. The tips of my fingers started to tingle as I watched Roxy and Sanders.

"Those two seem to have really hit it off." Jack appeared at my side, his arm brushing against mine.

The panic in me fizzled out where our bodies grazed. I quickly tore my focus away from where I'd been caught staring. I grunted some sort of response.

"The bus is ready. Are you?" He nudged me gently.

I looked up to him and this time my breath was taken away for a different reason. I always forgot how handsome he was until I saw him again. His normal easy smile wasn't there but his hair was shaved closer to his head and the beard across his jaw was edged to a clean line. He wore a black fleece vest over a gray long-sleeved tee that made his arms look ripped. For a math professor he had the body of an athlete.

His brows lifted as he waited for me to respond.

"Uh, yeah. All set."

"Here." He handed me one of the two to-go cups of coffee he held. "I got it like you like your men."

I was so shocked at the passing comment, dropped like a bomb, that I couldn't do anything but swallow as I took the steaming cup. Had I been that obvious in my ogling of him? Was that a joke? Would it be offensive if I laughed?

"Blond roast with cream and sugar," he said before turning sharply and heading to the bus.

My jaw hung open as I watched him jump up the steep bus steps in two easy hops. What the hell was that supposed to mean? I closed my mouth and flicked a glance around before following him. I took another deep steadying breath as I prepared for the trip ahead.

Joke was on him though. Typically I took my coffee hot and black.

CHAPTER 7

JACK

I was such an idiot. Stopped and got William coffee like a damn lovesick teen only to have found him mooning over Sanders. Un-fucking-believable. I kept telling myself I wouldn't give in to this crush but there I went going out of my way to help him again.

I stomped toward the bus full of drowsy teens. They ranged in ages from fifteen to seventeen, except one who just turned eighteen, but they all acted much older. Life had a way of aging some kids more than others. Early mornings were a lot to ask from them but at least hopefully they'd be chill on the drive up to the campsite. I felt, rather than saw, William join me at the front of the bus.

"Yo, listen up. Pause your Beats for two seconds," I said and waited for the group to obey. "Hey! Derek. Headphones." Ethan leaned across the aisle to shove the oblivious kid. He glared, looked up at me and slowly lowered them down. Derek had another black eye that I would be asking about later, but pretended not to notice before he quickly turned back into his hoodie. The bass from his headphones was still thumping loud enough to be heard all the way from the front.

As mad as I was with William, or rather frustrated with the situation and myself, I didn't want the guys to dislike him. If they sensed even for a second that I harbored any ill will for William, they'd make the next two

45

days miserable for him. After all, it wasn't William's fault he was a dumbass that fell in love with his straight best friend.

"This here is William. William is giving up his time to hang out with us and teach us cool shit. So don't be assholes. William, these are all the guys." Beside me, William stood silent, arms folded across his broad chest. He gave one silent nod, looking at each and every one of the kids. A few of the guys' eyebrows shot up and shared looks after giving William the once-over. He, at least, looked imposing as fuck.

"You can chat with him more when we get to the site but we gotta get going," I finished. "Now go back to bed, Sleeping Beauties. We'll be there in about two hours."

I was met with a chorus of grumbled affirmatives as headphones and earbuds were replaced. It was a full-size school bus, so the front seats were filled with all the camping supplies as the guys took up the back few rows. There were only ten of them that could come on this trip but it meant they got their own seats, so they lounged on their packs, hooded heads against the windows, and promptly went back to sleep.

I gave the bus driver the go-ahead and we were off.

I sat down next to William, and with a lowered voice said, "I know that wasn't the warmest reception but trust me it's better to let them rest for now. They aren't human yet. I'll introduce you to each one of them when they've had their Red Bull or whatever shit they pump into their veins nowadays."

William's gaze flicked to the free seat across the aisle and then back to me. "I thought we should go over the plan for the next few days," I said as explanation for crowding his space.

William nodded but his color was a little pale. Despite myself, I felt for him. I already knew him well enough to recognize that the more silent he was, the more his nerves had gotten the best of him. He came into this blind. These were good kids but any group of young people could seem like a wild pack of animals to a stranger. He blinked slowly and yawned so big I could see a filling in his molar. So maybe a little bit of nerves and also not a morning person? I shoved a paper bag onto his lap with *Daisy's* stamped on the side. The smell of sweet and fried goodness wafted my way.

"Don't let the heathens see or we'll be swarmed. These doughnuts are a favorite from a local diner called Daisy's Nuthouse in Green Valley. People come from all over to get—"

I was cut short by the speed in which he inhaled the sprinkled doughnut he had selected out of the bag. Before I had even finished the sentence, he had taken down the entire thing in three bites. I couldn't help but appreciate the fine tendons and muscles that worked the food in his mouth. He swallowed loudly before licking his lips.

"What?"

"You don't waste any time," I said, indicating to the empty napkin in his hand.

He shrugged. "They're really good. Thank you. And thank you for the coffee." He took a long drink and grimaced.

"Too sweet?" I asked with innocence.

"It's fine. I just usually take it without anything." He flicked a glance to me and then away.

"Noted." I would not be reading into that. Not after I made that asinine comment back at the Lodge when I was pissed off.

"So you wanted to talk?" He drained the coffee and tossed the empty cup into the trash can up front by the driver. He tucked his hands under his arms and slouched into the seat until he could comfortably lean his head back. Chugging that coffee down had zero impact on him. He yawned again, covering his mouth with the back of his hand.

"We can wait if you want to sleep too," I said.

"No, no. I'm good," he said. Before yawning. Again.

"Well, I assumed we'd set up the tents as soon as we got there." As I spoke, William locked his focus on me but he blinked rapidly and his head kept jerking. I recognized this from students who were on the brink of sleep. "Then we could find the local rhinos to ride. You just have to tickle their nipples and they really go for it."

William's head jerked again, his lids hardly open. "Mm-hmm."

He was so far gone. I kept talking knowing that the lull of my deep voice would trip him over the edge into dreamland. I made my voice even more monotone until his eyes closed completely. His jaw went slack and he softly snored. Even his snores were unobtrusive.

47

I let out a long sigh and pulled out my phone. The bus made a sharp left turn causing William to fall onto me until his head rested on my shoulder.

He smelled like hotel soap and fresh sheets. I rolled my eyes at myself.

I should shove him off. Instead I pulled out my phone and took a selfie in which I look annoyed and William's mouth hung open, seconds from drooling. I sent it to Ford and Suzie with the caption, "Must be my captivating conversation."

"Aww, so comfy," Suzie replied instantly.

Ford typed and typed. I locked my phone and let out a breath. There were plenty of things I could be working on. Articles and papers I'd been meaning to read. Instead, I leaned back. I allowed myself to enjoy this moment. It wouldn't last forever and it was nice. He was warm and solid and sexy. It was just nice to be close to someone.

Someone I wouldn't let myself fall for.

Ford's response buzzed in my pocket. "Are you sure that he is enamored with somebody else?" Only Ford took the time to write full sentences and use words nobody else would ever text. Who even said enamored anymore?

And yet.

My heart began to race. I imagined lifting his chin, kissing him like we did that night. Except you know, without the bus full of kids.

I lost track of time and focused only on what I felt. His arms slackened and his big calloused hands fell, palms up, limp on to his lap. Such big, strong hands … *the better to stroke you with*. His flannel was rolled up to reveal hairy forearms that were thick with muscles even this relaxed. The heat from his sleeping body warmed my entire left side.

The bus bumped over a massive hole, waking half the guys.

"What the hell?"

"Was that a moose?"

A few of them grumbled.

William sat straight up, eyes still closed.

I stood up and turned around in the seat. "It was just a pothole." I motioned down with my palms and shushed the ones who woke up. They instantly fell back asleep. I was on a bus full of zombies.

When I looked down at William, his fuzzy gaze was locked on my ass.

Whether or not he was aware of it. I took the opportunity to adjust myself for no other reason than I wanted to see what he'd do. His gaze remained focused on my lower half. He swallowed.

When I turned to sit back down, he blinked himself out of his stupor.

"Did I fall asleep?" He looked around befuddled, pulling out his phone. "What time is it? How long until we get there?"

I fought the smile that so badly wanted to come out. He was like a confused little puppy.

"Stop looking at me like that." His intimidating grumble was lost on his fuzzy bedhead.

"Like what?"

"Like you think I'm adorable."

I shrugged innocently.

He was adorable. I didn't want to think about how nice it felt to have him drowsing on my shoulder. I wouldn't let myself think about that. *Nope.*

"I didn't sleep well," he said.

Another bump caused his phone to fall to the floor. As he bent to pick it up, some cards in his back pocket slid out. I grabbed them and quickly examined the notes.

"What are these?" I asked as I read.

Some were just bullet points that said things like "Build a fire" or "simple trap." Another had the list of all the guys on the bus. He had prepped for this trip.

"Nothing." He reached to snag the cards from me but I pulled them away from him, blocking him with one arm as I read.

"You did research," I said and then titled my head to read, "Why is this one about dabbing crossed out?"

He shook his head, his cheeks were bright red.

"You looked up all the kids coming?" I looked at him now that he stopped struggling.

He looked around and whispered, "Ford gave me the roster. I thought I should at least know their names."

Despite my very logical mathematician brain, my heart pitter-pattered dangerously in my chest.

"You're doing it again," he grumbled.

"What?"

"Looking at me like I'm a fluffy bunny you want to take home and feed carrots to."

My cough of laughter surprised us both. He smiled at his clenched hands.

"This is very thoughtful," I said earnestly.

He scratched the back of his neck and shrugged. Every time he did that, I considered it an invitation to check out his body.

"It's important to me that I don't mess this up," he whispered.

"You won't. Just the fact that you made any effort at all means something."

He rubbed his eyes and sat up straighter. "Let's go over the plans now."

"Are you sure?" I asked though he did seem a lot more alert.

"That nap helped."

We spent the next hour chatting about the guys and making plans.

"I'm worried about Derek. He had a bruised eye again," I admitted.

William's brow furrowed. "I saw that too."

"He and Ethan clash like crazy. He likes to pick fights. But I think he gets it from his father."

William's frown deepened. He swallowed. "My dad hit me too. It's why I went to live with William and Sanders."

"I'm sorry," I said. I had assumed his home life was shit.

"But he needs to stop the cycle." He flicked a look to me.

"I agree." I didn't like giving a bad impression of the guys. They were here because Ford and I had faith in them. "They're mostly good kids. Anytime they're dicks, it's only because they're trying to act like some movie idea of what masculinity is."

"People just need someone to believe in them," he said.

"Exactly." I was getting worked up. "Just one person to tell them that they have it within them to do whatever it is that gives their soul life. And that it doesn't make them bad or dumb or weird. They just need to be told they are capable. It can change the whole trajectory of life. To have someone believe in you." I felt the fervor in my voice. This was so important to me. The reflected fire in his eyes told me that he understood that.

"I had that." His voice was slow and measured. He struggled to find the words now. He was on the brink of emotion. "That was what William gave me. A person who told me I wasn't a piece of shit. Sanders treated me like a human when the rest of the school treated me like a freak." His eyes grew fuzzy as he replayed memories of his past. "Sanders has always accepted me as I am."

"You love that family a lot."

He nodded. My anger towards Sanders was misplaced. I didn't know their history. Many people didn't understand the friendship between Ford and me because they didn't know the harsh history that bound us. We were battle brothers. And so were Sanders and William. I would never know the depth of their connection. I had to be okay with that. And okay, Sanders wasn't a total dick but couldn't he see how William felt about him? Wasn't it obvious? If anybody ever looked at me like that …

"I'm glad I'm here," he said, finding my gaze and interrupting my thoughts.

"Me too," I answered honestly.

* * *

William

THE BUS ROLLED to the campsite, the air brakes releasing with a loud hiss. Jack and I were the first ones standing.

"Up and at 'em. Grab as much as you can on your way out," Jack instructed.

The guys roused and grumbled into action. The door opened letting in the smell of a heated engine and the summer day. The campsite was secluded enough and bumped up against a forest-lined lake. It was beautiful. The trees went for miles fading into a haze that must be the reason they are called the Smokies.

I hauled some tents to the side when I sensed something up ahead. A kid, Ethan, I think was his name, was trying to hide his phone behind his back. He had gauged ears and a beanie that looked like it was going to pop off his head at any minute. Did he know it was eighty degrees with at least that much percentage of humidity?

"Look at that ass," one of the other guys said as he bent to look at the screen Ethan had been trying to hide.

Derek, the one with the bruised eye, pushed past him, shoving Ethan's shoulder roughly so that his phone fell to the ground.

"Cool it," Jack warned them both.

Another guy picked it up and said, "Yo, damn!" covering his mouth.

Ethan snatched the phone back but not before I caught enough of skin flashing to step forward without thinking. My defenses were raised but I wanted to keep myself cool until I had the facts. It wasn't easy.

"That your girl?" I asked Ethan.

The kid cleared his throat and looked up at me and around where a few guys stood watching. His eyebrows rose for a minute before he slipped into his tough-guy demeanor again. "Uh, nah. Can't tie me down." His gaze flicked to Derek who glared from a distance.

I stared straight into Ethan's eyes. "This her Instagram?"

"Nah, man. These were sent right to me." He made his voice higher, pretending to be a girl. "She said she's gonna miss me."

"She tell you you could share these?"

His gaze flicked to his friends who suddenly couldn't make eye contact anymore. I kept my face neutral but my blood was pumping now. Jack was helping the rest of the guys unload the bus but he shot a questioning look to me. I shook my head once.

Ethan swallowed and lifted his chin. "She didn't tell me not to."

"Are you bragging about sexual assault?" I asked.

"Come on." He rolled his eyes. "She sent them to me. I didn't make her."

"She tell you she's cool with other guys seeing her?" I asked, my voice was low with warning.

A few more guys stopped what they were doing to eavesdrop but I didn't move my oppressive glare from Ethan.

"I get you're the new guy and want to come off as a badass, but this ain't none of your business, Brawny Man."

I flexed my jaw and Jack came forward. "What's going on?" he asked looking between Ethan and me.

"This tough guy is sharing child porn on his phone," I said.

A few guys gasped and said, "Oh shit."

"Jesus, bro. It's not child porn." Ethan's cheeks grew ruddy. He glanced around. Derek was leaning against a nearby tree with his headphones on and hood up but watched the interaction closely.

"She eighteen?" I asked.

His glare was answer enough. "She's the one that took them and sent them to me. Not my fault. She should know better."

I must have flexed my fists because Jack put a hand on my arm and I relaxed back. "Do you really think that?" I asked the kid. "Think about this girl who trusts you enough to share these with you. Think about how she would feel to know this. Does it feel good?"

Ethan swallowed and his shoulders dropped. "I wasn't sharing them. I just opened my phone and there they were."

I believed him but he was posturing and I had a point to make. "You feel like a big man now? Huh?" I crossed my arms, flexing my biceps and stepped closer.

"Shit. It isn't that big of a deal."

"It is a big deal. You're eighteen and she's not. If I see you sharing anything like this again, I'll take your shiny new iPhone and throw it in the fucking lake. You feel me?"

Ethan glowered, face burning. I stepped forward and he flinched back. I lowered my voice and whispered in his face. "You don't need to be that guy. You're better than that."

His jaw worked as he ground his teeth. "Shit. Fine."

He stomped away and into the trees. Derek followed him a second later.

I looked to Jack who had an eyebrow raised at me. I lifted and dropped a shoulder.

"Let's finish unloading so the driver can hit the road," Jack called out and the guys got back to work, pulling out their tents and setting them up. I felt them looking me up and down as they worked.

"Well, that got their attention," Jack said quietly after coming to my side.

"Sorry about that," I said.

"No. It was good to see. And you were right. Ethan is better than that," he said frowning.

I was about to tell him that I'd seen the looks he and Derek shared. I knew those looks. The secrecy. He was just trying to prove something he didn't need to, but that wasn't my news to share.

When Jack looked up again, he frowned and tilted his head.

"You okay?" he asked, stepping closer.

The bus driver came down off the bus with a newspaper under his arm, walking in between us, forcing us to step back and apart. "I'm gonna hit the head and walk around for a bit before I get back on the road. I'll be back in twenty." He smacked the paper against his palm and walked away.

"Bathrooms?" I asked.

"And showers." Jack rolled his eyes. "It was the only way I could get half of them to agree to come. It's more like an introduction to camping."

"It's glamping," I said. I had envisioned more of a backpacking/hiking excursion. Were we really going to be in one spot the whole time? Did we have a chef? Jesus, was there Wi-Fi up here? "I was lucky to even have a sleeping bag growing up," I grumbled.

"Did you also walk two miles to school, uphill both ways?" His eyes twinkled.

I glared to fight the smile.

"But seriously, come here." He grabbed my wrist and pulled me on the bus, grabbing a first aid kit as he went.

I frowned as he pushed me gently into a seat.

"What?"

"You're bleeding, Brawny Man."

I raised an eyebrow at the new nickname. I lifted a hand to my lip and it came back with a spot of blood. "Damn."

"Here, let me see." He kneeled in front of me. "Don't forget I'm first aid trained."

He grabbed my jaw, turning it side to side to examine my mouth. I held my breath as I watched him.

"I run an adventure company," I said. "I am too."

"Hmm." Jack ran his thumb along my bottom lip. I felt it even if I couldn't *feel* it. It buzzed through my chest and down my spine. I swallowed. His face was so close to mine I could see the different facets of his rich brown eyes. He licked his full lips and I fought to keep my body under control. "Well, then you should really know when you're bleeding," he spoke softly.

My ears burned. "I can't feel my lip at that spot. I have nerve damage. Sometimes when I talk too fast, I bite it without realizing."

I didn't often admit that to people, anybody really. But I didn't want him to think I was an idiot either who couldn't speak properly. "It must have happened when I went off on Ethan," I added.

"Can you not feel it?" he asked as he dabbed it with a cotton pad. I shouldn't let him baby me like this. I was fine to take care of myself. But I couldn't bring him to stop either. Not when he smelled so damn good and it felt so nice to be taken care of.

The bus was heating from the midday sun without the AC flowing. The way it had been parked, blocked us from the site where the guys were setting up tents. Still. This was reckless. He made me reckless.

I shook my head and doing so caused his thumb to rub the middle part of my lip where my nerves were very much alive and well. Electricity shot through me. So I hadn't been drunk or confused that night at the bar. This attraction between us was explosive and unpredictable.

I felt it when I woke up to find that I had fallen asleep on him on the drive up. I felt it looking at his ass. I felt it just thinking about being next to him. It was undeniable.

"We should probably go back," I said.

"Yeah." Jack's eyelids grew heavy as his gaze moved over my face, his lips were closer than they had been.

We stared at each other without moving. My breaths grew faster. My fingers itched to pull him and kiss him like that night.

Then someone yelled, "Fight!"

Jack and I were off the bus and not a moment too soon. Any longer and I couldn't imagine what would have happened next. What I would have done to him. No, actually, I could imagine it. I easily imagined it.

Jack ran to where the crowd of guys had formed a circle, easily busting through. I was a second behind him. He pulled off Derek who was currently pummeling Ethan's face. I grabbed Ethan and pulled him away and to a stand.

Jack and I shared a look.

Everything was off to a fantastic start. This was going to be a great trip. Nothing to worry about at all.

CHAPTER 8

JACK

"She's my sister. You piece of shit!" Derek screamed as I held him back with difficulty.

They were kids but they were tough as shit and Derek especially knew too much about fighting.

Ethan ran a hand over his face, where William held him a few feet away. "I'm bleeding! You asshole!"

"How will you get your modeling contract now?" Derek rolled his eyes and I had to agree.

It was bad enough he was worried about his face when he had been looking at pictures of Derek's sister. William ground his jaw and I worried it wasn't any better having Ethan in his hands.

"Ethan. Delete those pictures. You're better than that," I said low and demanding.

Ethan had the decency to look ashamed. "It's not like I told her to send them," he mumbled, then quickly said, "Ouch." He shot a look of indignation to William who remained passive.

"I slipped," William said.

"Fuck. If I knew it was gonna be like this, I wouldn't have agreed to come on this bullshit trip." He shrugged out of William's hold. He took out his phone and made a few motions. "There, deleted. Happy?"

"You cooled down now?" I asked Derek.

He nodded once, jaw clenched tight. I let the kid go when I was sure he wouldn't go at him again.

"You two need to figure your shit out. We won't put up with this BS this whole trip."

"I'm going to the bathroom." Ethan shoved away in the direction of the bathroom.

"You wanna talk about what's going on?" I asked Derek quietly, glancing at his bruised eye. His dark gaze bore into me, the bruised one of his eyes was bloodshot.

He shook his head before he too walked away. I sighed. He'd talk when he was ready. For all his gruffness, he was highly sensitive. As always, I shot a glance to William who watched that interaction closely.

"Let's finish setting up the tents," I said to the others. "Then everybody go swim in the lake to cool off."

"Don't forget sunscreen," added William. He pulled out a few bottles of 50 SPF sunscreen out of his backpack and tossed them around.

I raised my eyebrows in surprise.

"What? They'll burn," he said.

"You're right. Now you can check that off your list." He flushed as I stepped closer. "You remembered everything, didn't you?"

At that, his gaze moved over my shoulders and he paled. "Oh shit."

In a flash he hopped back on the bus. I watched him race up the aisle, checking under the seats. He walked off the bus running his hands through his hair.

"What?" I asked growing more concerned.

He was mumbling under his breath. He was so worked up that he bit his lip again but this time he did it hard enough that he must have tasted the blood on the inside because he flinched and immediately touched his mouth. "Shit," he swore angrier now.

"Hey, it's okay." I rubbed his shoulder with my thumb, trying to calm him down from panic that seemed to quickly be growing. His lip was slightly swollen and he tongued it.

He took a deep breath in and out. "I forgot a tent." He looked away.

My heart skipped. "Oh. That's no biggie. Mine is a two person."

He looked back at me and held my gaze with a knowing look. Like I wasn't realizing the biggest issue. So the heat between us was as tangible for him as it was for me?

"It will be fine. You can be big spoon," I teased.

His eyes widened. "I—"

"Jesus, William, I'm kidding. It's really not that big of a deal." I told the lie smoothly even though my heart was racing. Could I handle two nights with him? Absolutely. Would I wake up with a massive boner for him. Also yes. But I was a grown-up and it had to be fine.

"What about the guys? Will they care?" he asked.

I waved away his concerns. "No. Half of them are sharing tents. Plus they are self-absorbed teenagers. They won't even notice unless we make a big deal about it."

William nodded and his Adam's apple bobbed on a hard swallow. "Okay."

"Seriously. No worries."

He continued to fiddle with his lip.

"And stop doing that." I thumbed his chin and he stopped. "If you don't stop tonguing it, it won't go down."

His gaze flicked up to mine. His nostrils flared.

Yes. That was definitely the best phrasing. Way to go, Jack.

"Let's make sure the tents are all set up and staked so they don't blow away with the first breeze," I said.

He chuckled and rubbed the back of his neck. "I seriously cannot believe I forgot it."

"I know. It was the first item on your list," I teased.

He grumbled and lightly bumped into me as we made our way to the tent area.

"As long as you got the food, we're fine," I said.

He stopped suddenly. This time his color drained so fast I felt too bad to go on.

"I'm kidding. I'm sorry, I'm sorry," I said between laughter.

"Too soon," he said. This time, when he shoved me, I almost fell over.

* * *

WE RESERVED two campsites next to a large lake. Ford had figured the guys would like the illusion of a little more freedom. A large flat cement pad with a grill and picnic table separated the two sites, giving us all plenty of space from each other. Thankfully the bathrooms, with showers, were only a short walk away. I had to admit it was nice. William seemed like he'd been looking forward to a few days of backpacking Bear Grylls–style but I wasn't about that life. It was bad enough I only had a foam pad and sleeping bag to sleep on. I already wanted to take a shower to get the dirt out from in between my toes.

The guys set up their tents as far away from us as they possibly could. These guys would be up way later than I could hang and I didn't want to be kept up by them. Is this what being in my thirties meant?

As the guys came back from their swim, many of them shivered and hopped around. It had been a hot day, but as the sun crept down behind the tall pines, the temperature dropped fast.

"Since it's already getting late, we're gonna make dinner and hang out the rest of tonight. Tomorrow we hike to the falls," I announced as the guys pulled their hoodies on and shivered.

William went to the fire pit and crouched in front of it.

"Is that dryer lint?" Ethan asked.

William replaced the tiny bag he'd taken the dryer lint out of. Okay, I had to admit even I was confused. Then he pulled a knife from his pocket and flicked it open, glancing at Ethan as he did.

"I was just asking." He threw up his hands. His thin pale frame was covered with goose bumps.

"Maybe put on a shirt," I suggested.

"And rob everybody of this view?" He kissed his tiny flexed bicep with blue shivering lips. Had to admire his confidence.

Derek threw a blanket at Ethan. They seemed to have gotten their aggression for each other out in the lake at least.

I brought my focus back to William as he bent over his task. The large muscles of his back strained at the shoulders of his flannel. His mouth was in a tight line of concentration as he focused on his task. The rest of the guys came around with their folding chairs to set up around the circular rock fire pit.

William lifted his chin, eyes focused as he checked the air for something. A light breeze blew a few strands of his hair back. After a second, he shifted around to the other side of the pit so his back was no longer to me. He dropped to his knees and leaned toward the fire pit. From the keys hanging from a carabiner on his hip, he lowered a small black rod to the pile of lint.

"This is a ferro rod." He held it firmly and quickly slid the blade of the knife down it.

A satisfying grinding sound was accompanied by a large flash of light. The little pile of lint immediately caught fire.

A few guys called out, "Whoa" and "No shit."

"This is the easiest way to start a fire, if you don't have a lighter. You want to gently grow the fire." He gingerly picked up the burning pile and laid it on a couple of thin sticks and bark. He softly blew on the flame, his lips pursing as he did so. His gaze flicked to mine as he worked. Awareness shot through me. My mind instantly imagined those lips doing very naughty things to me.

"Now get some super dry kindling. Make sure it gets lots of air. This light breeze is actually helping but any more might be a pain in the ass." He moved the fire around, having no fear of getting burned as he babied the flame to life.

Why the hell was this so hot? Thank God for the crowd, otherwise I might have done something embarrassing like drool over his raw masculinity.

"That's awesome. Can I try the stick thing?" Ethan asked.

William scooted over and patiently guided Ethan through the same process, holding no grudges from the earlier confrontation. If anything, he was extra calm and patient.

"Good," he encouraged.

Soon the fire was blazing bright. Ethan stood up and roared, raising his arms into the air. "I am man! Fire good. Where is my stick? I must cook meat!"

The others laughed at his show, even Derek pulled his hoodie up to cover his smile.

It was so incredibly hot watching William build a fire and work with the guys. He let all that wanted to take turns. I even tried the little stick thing and marveled at the flying sparks.

The mood grew pleasant as we grilled sausages donated from a local Winston brother and the sun set casting us all in soft pink light. Contented with full bellies and a good day in the sun, the guys all got along well. The fire burned strong for hours. Eventually, Derek pulled out a guitar.

"If he plays *Wonderwall*, I'm leaving," William whispered into my ear from where he sat next to me in his camping chair.

I suppressed a shudder when his breath tickled my ear. "I doubt any of these guys even know that song."

His eyebrows shot up when the familiar chords to *Times Like These* filled the air. William mirrored my surprise. "I stand corrected." Then louder I clapped and said, "Great song," to Derek.

He nodded with a secret grin as he started singing the soulful lyrics.

"Old school," someone else shouted.

"Ouch," William said.

"Foo Fighters are old school? Y'all wound me," I put a hand to my chest.

The laughter dimmed as we all grew rapt watching Derek sing. His voice was deep and guttural. He sounded like Dermot Kennedy but his lip curled and his eyebrows pursed with all the angst of an emo rocker. He was going to break a lot of hearts, this one. I knew he was a musician but I had no idea he was so talented.

Ethan watched him with intensity I'd never seen in the joker. It was all making sense in that moment. When Derek sang about being divided and deciding whether to stay, Ethan slid up his hood and leaned back, hiding his face, and stuffing his hands deep in the pouch.

I snuck a glance to William who watched, his eyes almost closed as he gently rocked to the music. He glanced over as though he felt me watching and gave me a sleepy smile. My heart raced away.

This guy. He was going to get me to do something very stupid.

"I'm going to shower and then bed." I stood suddenly.

"Lame," someone shouted.

"I know. I'm old and all your youth-ing about has tired me out." I stretched. "Don't stay up too late. We start the hike early. No booze. No weed. I'm dead serious. If I catch one sniff of either, you're out of the program. I'm not kidding. What you guys do on your own time is your choice, but when we are in charge of you, no fucking around."

I glared at each of them around the fire. Triple F—dammit, Ford, now I was calling it that—was on thin ice because of the nature of the students in the program; the last thing we needed was to be booted out of the site. I wasn't actually worried though. They knew we were all lucky to be able to do these sorts of outings and wouldn't want to ruin it. Still, I had to play the adult.

"Clear?" I asked loudly.

"Crystal," they called back.

"I'll stay up a little while to make sure the fire is put out properly," William said. He didn't look up at me. Which I was actually relieved about. Regardless of how I assured him, it felt like he was still being weird about the tent thing. Now I could pretend to be asleep when he finally came to bed.

And pretending it would be, because there was no way I was sleeping with that man next to me.

CHAPTER 9

WILLIAM

*T*he light of the lantern floated from the tent and off towards the bathrooms. I was as tired as Jack had seemed but I was waiting another hour at least. The fire was a weak excuse when really I wanted to make sure there was no chance I'd walk in on him changing for bed. I wanted him to be asleep by the time I got to the tent. It was getting harder to ignore my attraction to him. Two nights in a tent was feeling more like an impossibility. And it was all my own stupid fault. I couldn't believe I forgot a tent. It was on the list. I swore I had it with my stuff to be loaded.

I picked up a thick stick and used my knife to whittle it to a sharp tip. I passed it over to the left so the guys could roast marshmallows.

Jack's gaze as he touched my lips, as he watched me stoke the fire, kept appearing in my head. I knew that look. We had to be careful.

"He can't hear you, he's lost in thought." Ethan called out, "Yo, Brawny Man."

I blinked up, belatedly realizing they had been talking to me.

"What's up?" I asked, my voice even more grumbly from the smoke and not talking.

"We asked if you were married," Kyle asked. He was a short kid with a ton of brown hair he constantly shook forward into his eyes and then brushing away.

"No," I said.

"Girlfriend?" someone I couldn't see on the other side of the fire asked.

"Nope." The blade of the knife shucked off a large curl of wood. I squinted up. "No boyfriend either."

"I told you," Ethan said and I tensed. "He's a total lone wolf."

I relaxed my shoulders. Jack had told me that kids today—did I really just call them that?—didn't give a shit about who you dated, but being around a group of teens had me on edge like I was fifteen again.

"I have dated. Just not currently," I clarified.

"High standards?"

"Commitment phobia?"

"Daddy issues?"

The questions all came back-to-back from the circle and I just shook my head laughing. "We aren't having this conversation."

"But you can help Dom though, right?" Ethan asked. "With his lady problems."

"Shit, man." The guy in question, Dominic, was wearing matching gray sweats and wore a beanie so low I almost couldn't see his eyes. He had the makings of a mustache that was trying really hard to be full grown. "I don't need no help. My woman has no complaints." He threw a marshmallow at Ethan who grabbed it out of the air and chewed it with enthusiasm.

"I hope that's true," I said, still focused on my task.

Dominic leaned forward. "What's that supposed to mean?"

"Just what I said. I hope that you talked to her and she's satisfied."

Dominic leaned back, legs spread wide, foot tapping. "I don't need to ask her." He lifted his chin in challenge.

I held his gaze as I ran the blade over the stick. "Yes. You do."

"He thinks she's faking her O's to get him to finish," Ethan offered happily.

I gave him an exacerbated look. This kid really wanted his ass kicked.

"Shit, man. Shut up. I didn't say that." Dominic smoothed his "mustache."

"What did she say? When you asked her what she liked?" I asked him.

His gaze moved to the fire avoiding my question. I looked around the fire. "You guys are asking your partners, right? If you're fooling around, then you better be talking."

When none of them responded. I sighed loudly and threw the newest stick hard, to spear it into the ground. "Alright. I'm only gonna say this once and you guys need to really listen."

"We've had the birds and bees talk, Brawny Man." Derek spoke up for the first time in a while.

I scratched at my beard. "Oh yeah? What? Wear a condom? Don't get her pregnant? Beware of STDs?"

"Nah, dog, we know about consent and all that shit," Dominic said defensively.

"All that shit?" I said it so sharply the group went quiet. "Consent is the bare minimum. Enthusiastic consent, that's the aim." I shook my head when all I received were blank stares and open mouths. "How do you expect to be men if you don't know this 'shit'?"

A few of them grumbled.

"No. You wanna talk like real men? This is how *real* men talk. Consent is the absolute lowest standard you're going for." The vehemence in my voice surprised me. For being the most understanding and open generation, they treated sex like a badge to be earned and I was pissed. Women especially weren't objects and this type of talk needed to end now.

"Any prick can get a person who's half out of her mind. Or guilt them into sex because they think they're owed something. It takes a real connection to sweep someone off their feet and get them ready to go. You understand that?" I asked.

"So how do we do that?" Kyle asked with a flick of his bangs.

"You talk to your partners. You listen to them. You explore them and touch them where they want to be touched. You better be willing to work. You get them so worked up they're begging for it."

A few "hells yes" bust out of the group. I paused speaking because I worried I would bite my lip again. I took a deep breath and lowered my shoulders.

"And until they're ready, it's your job to make them feel safe and wanted. Safe. And wanted. Anything less makes you a coward. Ain't nothing sexy about a man who uses his strength for anything other than stamina." I looked around at each and every one of them. "You get me?"

They nodded.

"You want to blow their mind. Enthusiastic consent. That's the goal. Anything else is fucking weak."

I sat back into my chair.

"Brawny Man has game," Ethan said.

"No. It's just way more fun when both parties are into it." I picked up another branch and began working it.

The guys made whooping noises. I wasn't sure if this was appropriate conversation with teenagers, but better than perpetuating these hurtful ideals of what masculinity means. I didn't think I could have said all that with Jack next to me. I already fought the images that popped up thinking about getting him so worked up he was begging for it.

"Oh snap. Okay, okay," Ethan said. "I feel ya."

"You're good fucking people. You guys really have the potential to make a better future," I said. Emotion made my throat tight unexpectedly. "It's powerful."

They were quiet, but when I glanced up, they were nodding or staring at the fire. When I met Derek's gaze, his eyes were bright, nostrils flared.

"Be better men than our dads," Derek said quietly.

Chills ran down my arms. I held his gaze and my hand ran over the scar on my chin without thinking.

"You already are," I said softly.

* * *

THE CONVERSATION FLOWED to one topic and another. I zoned out not understanding half the shit they even talked about as I stared at the stars. It had been so long since I camped like this. Since I was still. It made my chest ache with memories. I thought of all the camping trips before I moved in with Sanders and William. So many inside jokes and stupid accidents we laughed about later. Those trips were my perfect oasis before returning to the hell of reality. I closed my eyes and fought back the emotions thinking of my surrogate father. I missed him so much. He was so far gone at the end. It broke my heart. But I was so thankful for the time we had. I owed him so much.

After a little while longer, I yawned loudly and stood up with effort. It had been enough time. Jack should be asleep by now.

"I'm calling it." I kicked Ethan's shoe to get his attention. "Make sure the fire is all the way out before you go to bed?"

He looked around before pointing to his chest. "Me?"

"Ah, shit, call Smokey, this forest is about to burn to the ground," Kyle said.

I shot him a look and he held up his hands. "Just kidding, just kidding."

I looked back to Ethan. "I know you won't let that happen. Let the flames burn all the way down and then dump that on there." I pointed to a bucket of water. "No coals, no nothing. Makes sure you shovel the ash on top."

He straightened as I spoke. "Water. Ashes. Got it," he said with seriousness.

"I know you do." I nodded at him and then to the group said, "Good night, all."

They said their good nights and I made my way blindly back to the tent in the dark. Away from the fire it was much harder to see. I pulled out a small flashlight and quietly crept to the tent. I slowly unzipped it, kicking off my shoes before getting in.

I moved as quietly as I could, with the flashlight beam lowered.

"It's okay, I'm still awake." Soft lantern light flickered to life. "Here, so you can see," Jack said.

"Uh, thanks."

Jack leaned up on his elbow, he wore a white henley unbuttoned that seemed to glow against his dark skin. His eyes were heavy with sleep but he watched me closely.

"I hope we didn't keep you up." I was whispering for some reason. Something about being in a tent just mandated it.

"No. I couldn't sleep." He wouldn't look away and I didn't want to make a big deal about changing. I began to unbutton my outer shirt.

"I heard what you told them," he said. "About consent."

69

My hands stilled halfway through the buttons. "I hope that was okay. I wasn't—"

"It was good. They like being treated like adults." He still wouldn't look away. His face was hard to read in this light.

I continued to take my flannel off, leaving only my white undershirt, and tossed it to my corner of the tent.

"They're good kids. They're shockingly open. I don't feel like I talked about anything at that age." I chatted as I unbuttoned my hiking pants and dropped them. My hands shook a little under his scrutiny. I swore his nostrils flared in the low light. If he had thoughts about my boxer briefs, he kept it to himself. Goose bumps broke out over my skin. I knew from experience that if I tried to sleep in this insulted sleeping bag with too much clothing on, I'd strip in the night or wake up in a puddle of sweat.

"They just want someone to treat them like they're worthy of being listened to," Jack said.

I thought of how Ethan looked at me when I asked him to watch the fire, like he hadn't been expected to be responsible for anything for a long time.

"You're good with them." His voice was deep and rough with sleep and it shot straight to my dick. I quickly lowered to slide into the cocoon of my bag. "You had nothing to worry about."

"I built it up more in my head." As usual, I thought.

"It seems like most people have a hard time with teenagers because they project a lot of their own shit onto them from their past instead of seeing the person. But you're giving them a chance to be seen and heard and that's all they want," he explained.

It felt good. Talking with them, feeling like maybe I was actually helping them. Not just with the sex talk but all day. It felt important. I knew my work was important too, in its own way.

I lay on my back, studying the nylon material. Distantly, the voices of the guys bounced off the water, low and laughing.

"I'm gonna have to let them sleep in tomorrow, aren't I?" Jack sighed as he clicked off the lantern.

I smiled. He was so gentle with them. Tough too, but he genuinely cared about them. "They're not gonna be functional until noon at least," I said.

He didn't respond for so long I wondered if he finally fell asleep. "Where'd you learn so much about wilderness stuff? Fire starting and all that?" Jack asked, seemingly as unable to call it a night as me.

"William took Sanders and me camping a lot. Almost every weekend during summers or longer if he could get time off. He taught me everything he knew about it."

I smiled thinking about some of the happiest times of my life. Just the three of us in the beautiful Rockies, talking about anything and everything as we stared out into the stars.

"Is that how you and Sanders got started with Outside the Box?"

"Yeah. It seemed that we were always bound to be working outside in some capacity. There was a time—"

I hadn't meant to say that but something about the atmosphere of the quiet tent allowed secrets to be shared.

"What?" he prodded.

I swallowed. "I was just thinking, remembering really, that for a while I wanted to do something like Triple F," I said.

"Oh God, not you too," he mumbled.

"What?" I turned to lie on my side and face him in the dark.

"Nothing." I could hear him shuffling; when he spoke his voice was closer too. "Go on, please. I want to know."

"Just being out here, with these guys. I'm remembering that I wanted to be a part of something like this. Give back somehow. Feel involved in making a difference for the future. I know if I had stayed on the path I was born into, I wouldn't be here today."

"Same. I bounced from foster home to foster home for so long before Carol and Joe, the parents who raised Ford and me," Jack explained. "So what happened?" he asked gently. "Why corporate adventuring?"

I let out a long breath. "I don't know exactly. It just sort of morphed into that over time. It was just us at first. We needed to make money. Denver was booming like crazy, tons of new businesses with North Face–wearing granolas who wanted to bond with their employees."

He chuckled.

"I sound jaded. I'm not. I know we were lucky to have the success we did doing what we loved to do. But it's not …"

"Not where your heart is?" he finished.

"No," I admitted softly. "Sometimes I think …" I licked my lips and stopped. My heart began to race in the darkness. I felt like it was shaking the ground. I was about to confess something to him that I never told anybody. Not even fully admitted to myself.

"What?" His hand found mine in the darkness and squeezed. His fingers were warm and calloused and again I wondered if he lifted weights to get that body.

I found courage in his silent encouragement. "The business is in trouble. Sanders … isn't doing well. Losing his father the way he did, after having lost his mother so young. He's just so fragile. He made some mistakes with OTB. Other companies are popping up doing what we do with more funding and …" I let out a shaking breath. I couldn't believe I was admitting it. "Sometimes. I wish he would just let OTB go so I could move on."

There was silence. Did he think that I was a terrible person? Did he think I was betraying the man who helped me?

Eventually he cleared his throat. "You could leave. You don't have to stay just because it was his dream. Just because you have been a part of it. You're allowed to walk away too."

I couldn't explain that I couldn't abandon Sanders like that. He needed me. He didn't get the history. I settled on the easiest answer. "Sanders needs the help. I'm better at the back-end stuff. He's the face of the company."

Jack remained quiet.

"I shouldn't have said that," I said.

"Yes, you should have," he said before letting out a long sigh. "I'm glad you shared. I just worry you're selling yourself short. You were good today. If this is something you want to do. Or at least closer to it. You should give yourself permission to explore that."

My face flushed in the darkness. "I know. Maybe one day. Thank you."

Neither one of us bought my lip service. I couldn't shake the feeling that I had disappointed Jack somehow with this admission.

"Good night," Jack whispered, releasing my hand and turning away.

"Good night."

I lay on my back for hours, listening until Jack's breaths evened out and deepened. I listened until even the guys quieted. Eventually I drifted off to sleep allowing myself to dream about things I never thought I could and wishing I still held Jack's hand in mine.

CHAPTER 10

JACK

I woke covered in sweat. It took a minute to realize where I was. I lay still while I got my bearings. The soft sounds of water lapped against the shore. Birds trilled in the trees. Mosquitoes buzzed and bumped into the outside of the tent. There was no sounds from the guys. They must have still been sleeping.

The air was a heady smell of man and sweat …

My eyes shot open. The tent was bright with light. Just how late had I slept in? I didn't think I would be able to sleep at all. Especially not after hearing William talk to the guys about getting his partners to beg for it. I lay awake for too long imagining things I didn't have the right to. Mostly things I would beg for and ways he would get me to do it.

I didn't have to look down to know I sported morning wood. I picked up my watch to glance at the time. It was only 8 a.m. but the sun was full-on slanting on the tent, baking us like an oven. I'd pulled off my shirt at some point and now my back clung to the insulated nylon of the sleeping bag.

I looked down with worry but my drawers were still in place. I let out a sigh and let my head fall back.

"So hot," William grumbled next to me.

I glanced over to see him lying on his stomach, arms crossed under his head. His shirt had come off too at some point. A sheen of sweat glistened the skin of his muscular back. It was perfectly sculpted, the tendons drew my gaze lower and lower to where only those beautiful boxer briefs remained, highlighting his perfect, round ass.

"So hot," I agreed as I took him in.

He peeked up at me through his arms, eyes squinty with sleep.

I quickly looked away and turned to open a side flap facing the lake. That at least let the breeze off the water come through the screen. I looked out at the glassy surface of the water, inhaling the fresh air.

I lay back down trying to cool off my burning skin. He rolled on to his back in my periphery.

"What time is it?" His morning voice did insane things to me.

"Just after eight," I said.

"Damn. I didn't think I would sleep so hard." He stretched out a big yawn.

"Me neither," I said.

"The guys still asleep, I'm assuming."

"Yup."

"So bright," he moaned.

I would not look to see if he was hard. I would not look at his cock whatever state it was in.

My eyes moved without my control. Greedy, horny bastards.

Holy shit.

His erection strained, clearly outlined against the fabric. Not only were the thick veins apparent but there was a dark spot of dampness in the cotton near the tip. The elastic band could barely contain him. I pulled my gaze away as fast as I could but not fast enough. I'd seen enough to fuel my nights and showers for months to come. Pun intended. I risked a glance to his face, my heart racing. Thankfully, his arm was thrown over his eyes.

So I hadn't been caught. Good. Because I shouldn't have looked. I would not look again. I had more self-control than this. Okay. Deep breaths until this boner went down. Think of unsexy things.

William blowing on the fire. William on his knees before me. William's lips under my fingertips.

Shit.

No. I could just get away from him. Maybe I'd go to the showers and relieve myself. Again. That wouldn't be suspicious.

A shuddered sigh next to me pulled me from my plan making. Slowly, afraid to be caught staring at him again, I turned my head toward William. But he wasn't looking at me. Or rather he was very much looking at me. Just not my face. His eyebrows were furrowed in focus. His sleepy eyes flicked to my cock and away before coming back again. His bottom lip was in his mouth, tonguing the bump on the numb area. He looked as conflicted and in pain as I felt.

Any remaining sleepiness instantly vanished as my heart bounced madly in my chest. Blood rushed to my cock, causing it to jump.

His worried gaze shot immediately to mine. Afraid he would be ashamed and pretend he wasn't looking, I slowly rubbed my hand down my chest and toward my cock.

His nostrils flared and sweat glistened on his hairy, heaving chest. He watched me so closely, his focus jumping from my face, reading my mood, to my hand that moved lower and lower. A breeze blew through the tent, sending chills over my damp skin and hardening my nipples.

He noticed too. He groaned so softly I almost didn't hear it. My fingertips grazed over my nipples, shooting lightning straight down my spine. I teased myself as he watched before letting my hand continue its journey lower.

I let my hand fall onto my cock. I stroked up and down the length of myself just once. I was already so close. My balls were so high and tight I thought I might come embarrassingly fast. I had made the first move. I wouldn't push him. I wouldn't make a sound.

With his breath still coming fast, he kept my focus as his hand moved to his own cock in my periphery. I swallowed.

I couldn't keep locked on his face any longer. I watched as he dipped his thumb into the waistband. His hips lifted as he tugged the material down and he sprang free. He circled his shaft and slowly thrust up between the loop he created until he was pressed all the way down at his base, creating his own version of a cock ring. The skin was pulled so tight, his

77

dick so hard, the tip seeped. The angle showed off his strong, rounded ass as he strained straight up into the air.

"Fuck," I whispered.

His thumb circled back to the tip to grab the moisture there and spread it around the tip.

Much less elegantly, I tugged my drawers down just enough to pull myself free. His eyes widened as they took me in. The heat in that desperate gaze brought me closer to the edge. I began to stroke as I watched him do the same. Breaths coming fast. The sounds of skin on skin. The smell of our heated bodies. It was too fucking much.

I arched up, using my feet to kick the sleeping bag away, to lie flat on the much cooler padding underneath.

He scooted off of his sleeping bag too, bringing us closer together. Close enough that his arm bumped repeatedly against the left side of my body. I itched to take him with my free hand but instead I ran it up and down my own chest, wishing it was his. His free hand tugged his balls as he stroked. His greedy gaze couldn't settle on one place to look at me. His scruffy cheeks were high with color. Sweat dotted his forehead.

The padding underneath me slipped as I jerked myself, tilting me closer to him. His long, hairy leg bumped up against mine. I inhaled a sharp breath.

He groaned so low and deep I had to take a break to squeeze the base of my cock to keep from coming. I didn't want this to end. He pushed his leg harder against mine. I bit my lip and tossed my leg over his, pulling myself even closer to him. His hip was snug up next to me, my left thigh on top if his right. The strong muscles of his leg strained as he tensed beneath me. The furious way he tugged himself shook my whole body. I was so close, my entire body burned with the need to release. We were slick with sweat where we touched, sweat and hair combining to make hot friction I couldn't get enough of. I liked how we slid against each other. I wished I could climb on top of him and grind until we were both completely slippery and stated.

With that thought I lost control.

My head went back as I silently screamed through bared teeth. I came harder than I ever have. I was still pulsing when I looked down to watch him finish. His eyes burned as he watched me. He looked where I spilled and followed me a moment later, turning his head into the pillow to groan. The muscles of his neck strained and his whole body tensed as he released. Pulse after pulse, shot up his stomach almost all the way to his collarbone. It was the most beautiful and erotic thing I had ever been a part of.

We lay on our backs panting for several minutes.

"So hot," he softly repeated the sentiment from earlier.

"Unbelievably hot," I agreed.

I turned to him, full dimple mode on display. He smiled shyly back. Eventually I reached to the side and grabbed a package of moistened wipes I brought. I handed one over to him without looking.

"Thanks," he said.

After we cleaned up, I leaned up on one elbow to look at him. "I better get breakfast started or they might riot when they wake up."

He was sleepy and content. He looked up at me hesitantly. "They might be asleep for a while yet."

I couldn't help the way my heart tripped a beat with a happy hope. He lay on clasped fingers behind his head, face neutral with content. His hairy armpits, massive biceps, ripped lats and tight six-pack were out there all sexy-like on display. He was fucking gorgeous. He looked up at me.

I wanted to kiss him so bad. His gaze moved to my mouth. I started to lower my head to do just that when a familiar buzzing zipped past my ear. A mosquito landed right on my nose.

I pulled back and swatted it away. "How the hell did that bastard get in here?"

William sat up and grabbed my face. "What was it?"

"A mosquito." I rubbed my nose sullenly where I accidentally smacked myself.

"Aww." He leaned forward to kiss my nose. It was the most sweet and unexpected gesture from him. I couldn't react. What did that mean? I felt my hopes gaining traction. This heat was real, but maybe it wasn't just heat. My respect and understanding of him grew too. What if …

"You know, Sanders calls them mozzies. He hates them. They always ate him up too, because he's 'so sweet.' According to him," he added, rolling his eyes.

It was like someone dumped a bucket of ice water directly onto my head. How could he bring him up now? It's not that I was a jealous person but was he really thinking of his best friend, when we just … *How*?

I sat back, sure my emotions were painted all over my face.

He frowned. "I-I-I just meant. I was just trying to say you're sweet," he said.

Once again, my heart softened, never ever able to stay hard towards him. "I know. Thank you." I forced a smile and stood up. "I'm gonna go shower, then I'll come back and start the eggs and bacon."

He nodded. He probably felt rebuffed. We'd been about to kiss. I understood that he meant what he said to be sweet. But it didn't change the fact that he *was* thinking about Sanders. He would always be thinking about Sanders.

I would always be an afterthought. This was exactly the feeling I had been trying to avoid. No more of this. From here out, I'd harden myself against my feelings for William. They were strong. I could no longer deny it. But I didn't have to give in to them. I didn't have to make it any worse than it was going to be when he left back to Denver.

* * *

William

AT WHAT POINT would I learn to speak without shoving my foot directly into my mouth? We'd been about to kiss, I wanted to kiss him, so bad. Especially after … God, it was good. He was so sexy. And it was so *so* good. I could still feel the heat of him next to me and hear his stuttered breaths heavy with want. Feel his strong leg flexing as he impatiently shifted with the need to come. And then I went and said that. I explained what I meant and yet he still seemed so hurt.

Maybe because you brought up another man right after you had your dick out?

Fuck.

I hadn't meant anything and yet … the damage was done.

My thoughts were as jumbled in my head as they would be if I tried

to speak, so I just went to work. After bringing the fire back to life—
Ethan had made sure it was all the way out as far as I could see—I set to
making coffee. By the time the eggs were scrambled, the bacon crackled
loudly, wafting the smell around the site. It was enough to rouse they
guys. They stumbled like zombies from the tents towards the tantalizing
smells.

Jack didn't return until everybody was up. He pointedly ignored me.
My stomach was in knots wondering how I could fix things with him. I
finally felt like we had moved past the awkwardness of our first meeting
but it was like there was always a barrier between us that I couldn't see.

"We're gonna head out in about an hour. Make sure you have water and
good hiking shoes on," Jack said. He shot a look to Kyle who sported black
and white Jordans in pristine condition.

Kyle paled and ran to put on shoes he wouldn't mind getting dirty,
presumably.

Once we were all fed, loaded up with sunscreen and bug spray, we
made our way toward the trailhead.

"You lead the way, and I'll bring up the end," Jack said.

By all outward appearances he seemed normal enough but he wouldn't
quite hold my gaze or be next to me on purpose. I nodded and gathered the
guys around.

"This trail is roughly a five-mile trail round trip. We'll go as slow as
you need to but it does incline pretty steeply in parts." I hefted my pack
onto my back. "This is a pretty popular trail, so there shouldn't be any
dangerous wildlife. But that being said, it would be irresponsible to not
prepare you. There are bobcats, coyotes, and even black bears in these
mountains. If you see one, stop moving and let me know right away.
Chances are they will be more scared of us but I do have bear spray if
needed."

A few of the guys cast nervous glances at each other.

"For real? Bears?" Dominic asked.

I nodded seriously.

"I didn't sign up for this shit," he said.

"You did actually." Jack chuckled lightly as he patted Dominic's shoulder. "Let's head out."

I took the lead and headed to the trailhead. It became quickly evident that my pace would be too much.

"How much longer?" someone asked from behind me.

"We haven't started," I said without slowing down.

A few grumbles and moans of complaint met me in response.

The longer we walked, the more they complained. It didn't bother me. I heard grown men who owned Fortune 500 companies complain much more about far less activity. I just kept my eyes focused on the trail and ears pricked. Even though the trail was just us in the middle of the day in the middle of the week, I wasn't actually worried about bears. It had been fun to fuck with them. I glanced back to check on the team once we were about a mile in. I paused and everybody followed, panting softly.

"Water break," I said to Ethan who was right behind me, to my surprise. He was more serious today than before. Derek was behind him and the other guys were all in a line between Jack and me. I shot a questioning glance to Jack to check in. He gave me a thumbs-up and wiped his forehead with his sleeve.

"I'm tired," Kyle said. He attempted to fluff his sweaty hair. I'm sure he was really more concerned with the lack of volume than anything.

"Did anybody bring snacks?" another asked.

Someone else shouted that he had a cramp.

"Y'all aren't gonna need to worry about bears or anything else with all this whining," Jack said.

"We're about halfway to the falls," I said. "Just stop for a second."

Everybody looked at me. "Just be still. Listen. Smell. Feel."

They shot each other glances of hesitation.

"Stop thinking and bitching and you'll realize this feels good. It's a beautiful day. You have nowhere else to be," I said.

To emphasize my point, I closed my eyes and leaned my face to the sun. People were far more willing to look stupid if someone else did it first.

I took a deep breath in. It was a beautiful day. My heart thumped strongly with exertion. The air smelled of fresh pine and earth, mixed with the residual campfire smells permeating from my clothes. The forest was loud with birds and chattering squirrels.

"It's so easy to get caught up in all the bullshit of daily life. When you're out here, there's a whole other world." I spoke with my eyes still closed. It was easier to get across the points I wanted to make. "None of your problems matter out here. It's like watching the stars. It gives you perspective. We are just a blip in the radar of the universe. It's important to remember that."

I spoke to them but reminded myself too. I had to get out more on my own. I needed to find who I was and what I wanted away from Sanders and OTB. I opened my eyes and they immediately set on Jack.

He had his hands on his hips. His head tossed back to feel the sun and listen to the sounds of nature. I had to force myself to look away. Otherwise I was sure I could watch him all day long. I wasn't sure when my attraction to him got so out of control. The jerk-off session in the tent only intensified the already distracting lust constantly heating my veins.

I moved my gaze to the others. They had closed their eyes, to my surprise. Ethan, too, had his features relaxed, head tilted to listen. He looked much younger when he wasn't trying so damn hard all the time. Derek opened one eye to look at him but closed it again with a frown when he caught me noticing. I forgot these guys were just teens. Ethan was the oldest at eighteen but everyone seemed so much older most of the time. They had so much living ahead of them. So much pain and heartbreak. I understood about growing up too fast. Times like this I wish I could tell them to just slow down. It was already too late for them. The curious innocence of childhood once lost never returns.

My gaze moved to Jack again. He was watching me closely, even from all those yards away I could feel it. He smiled at me with such warmth I hoped that my faux pas from earlier was forgiven.

I guess it wasn't all heartache in store for them. There was also late nights with good conversation. Passionate love affairs. New food and travel. No. They were lucky. They had their whole lives ahead still.

I was still holding Jack's gaze when a loud crack of a twig came from the forest to my right. All at once twelve sets of eyes turned to the trees. Then they all looked to me, eyes wide with fear.

I lifted my hands to assure them it was probably nothing. Still I looked at our exit options if we needed to get away quickly. This part of the trail was narrow, only one person could walk at a time. There was a steep ravine to their left and the thicket of trees to their right. I faced them, and they watched me, waiting for what to do next.

There was another shift in the underbrush and a few pebbles rumbled to the ground from the higher ground and into the path.

Several sets of eyes widened. Dominic looked like he was seconds from booking it. I thought I even saw someone make the sign of the cross. There was no joking or complaining now. Just raw fear that set us all on edge. The rustling became louder, something big was headed our way. It would just be my luck to have the only bear attack in the history of OTB and Triple F.

I lifted my finger to my mouth. Dominic was pale and all of the guys had no pretense of artificial toughness. They were all scared shitless.

All at once, hell broke through. A massive buck came careening down the steep slope, he broke onto the trail separating me from the others.

I was forced to jump back to get out of the way just in time to avoid being trampled. The buck didn't stop until he was several yards below. When he finally stilled, he looked back up at us. He was fierce, and muscular, a beautiful specimen of an animal. His haunches twitched as he held himself on the incline. His massive antlers shifted as he looked around the forest and then back to the trail, ears pricked. My heart raced. I didn't know if bucks attacked, but if he did, I would jump forward and distract him. Jack stood on the defensive.

Nobody moved as more sounds followed. A moment later a beautiful doe stepped gracefully into the path. She stopped right in front of me. I could reach out and touch her with only a few steps. She seemed to take each one of us in. I took a cautious step back as I watched her. The others followed my lead in my periphery taking a few steps backwards to give the couple a wide berth. Her dark round eyes watched me cautiously for what felt like minutes, but probably only seconds. I held her gaze. There was something about the moment that felt like more. It shouldn't feel so strange and religious to come across a wild animal, but I felt sought out having her attention.

The buck huffed and her head shot back to him. Finally, she stepped down into the ravine, taking her time to descend.

I placed a hand to my chest and exhaled a breath I didn't know I held.

My heart was hammering under my hand. A few guys let out nervous chuckles and sighs.

That's when I noticed the couple didn't move on yet though.

Wait, I thought but it was too late.

A moment later, three fawns came stumbling through the trees. They hopped, half fell, onto the trail with their knobby knees, and awkward steps. They broke apart the group as they scrambled to catch up with their parents. Kyle fell to the ground, covering his head with clasped hands. Dominic yelled so loudly it scared the family of deer. The smallest-looking fawn had fallen onto the path and the yell caused him to scramble and kick. A few guys had to jump well back to avoid getting the brunt of it. As soon as it scrambled to its feet, it joined its family and they all galloped away faster than they appeared.

When the commotion stopped, and the sounds of the deer were long gone, I asked, "Everyone okay?"

Kyle stood up with a sniff and dusted himself off. "That was wild," he said.

Dominic half jumped and pulled his hat off in excitement. "Shit, yo, I thought we almost died."

The others laughed and shared their post-adrenaline enthusiasm. Ethan had jumped in front of Derek at some point in the commotion. He still pressed him into a boulder protecting his much larger frame with his own lean one. Ethan stepped forward, releasing Derek free from the cage of his body.

"You saved me from the babies," Derek said but smiled and looked up at Ethan through his lashes.

I searched for Jack to see if he caught the moment. That's when I noticed that Jack was no longer at the back of the pack.

"Jack!" I yelled and ran to the edge where he had been standing only moments before.

I looked down the steep ravine, palms sweating in contrast to the fear that made me feel cold.

"There he is!" Kyle yelled.

I followed the finger to a glimpse of hiking boot and the unmoving figure on the ground several yards down.

"Don't do anything until I know what he needs," I said to Ethan. He nodded back, mouth in a tight line of worry.

Without another thought, I started down the side of the mountain, half-falling on loose pine needles and pebbles.

He had to be okay. I had to make sure he was okay. If anything happened to him, I would never forgive myself.

CHAPTER 11

JACK

I groaned. I lay on my back afraid to move for several seconds. Once I had stopped falling, I didn't want to cause myself to go sliding further. The wind had been knocked out of me, but more than that, I was fine. Except for feeling like a total dumbass. I waited for my adrenaline to settle down so I could see if I was in any pain anywhere.

I took several deep breaths. My right knee burned and the cool air stinging my skin told me I ripped my pants. I lifted my head tentatively to look at my leg. Sure enough, the pants had ripped and there was blood on my knee. I relaxed my head back into the leaves. I was definitely going to need a shower.

Above, William called my name.

Oh God, so embarrassing. How was I going to explain that I just tripped and fell over the edge because of the sweet tiny fawn?

Scared to death by baby Bambi.

If Ford ever found out about this, I would never hear the end of it.

I started to shift, but the less my heart raced, the more my other ankle hurt. Shit.

A few moments later, William was at my side. His eyes were wide, brows furrowed and his color was pale.

"Jack," he said my name on an exhale when he slid to a stop above me. He held on to a sapling to keep from sliding. "Are you okay?"

"Yes," I said.

His eyes moved up and down my body. "You're bleeding. How's your neck? Do we need to get an airlift?"

I moved to sit up. "No. I'm fine. I mean. Except the bleeding. And maybe my ankle. Definitely pride."

William crouched down to wrap his arm around my waist and helped me scoot up. "On a scale of one to ten, what is this embarrassment level? One being somewhere around saying 'you too' to a server who tells you to have a good meal. And ten being having a panic attack at a drag show and having a sexy stranger having to help you."

Haloed in the light, standing tall above me, he looked like my own personal superhero.

"Well, when you put it that way, a solid five," I said.

"You're gonna be fine."

We shared a smile as he lifted me to my feet.

"Go slow. The second something hurts, tell me."

I nodded and leaned into him maybe a little more than I needed to. Having his strong arms lift most of my body weight was nice and I really wasn't as bad as I—

"Oh ow, ow, shit," I gasped out.

"Your ankle?"

I winced and nodded as I tried to put more weight on it.

"Do you think you broke it?" he asked tightly.

"No. I think I would be screaming if it were broken."

"Hmm," he said and lowered me back to the ground.

I should insist that I'm fine but honestly his fussing over me felt nice. Selfishly I wanted to be the center of attention always in his life.

I shook away that wild thought.

"Let me look at it?" he asked but was already untying the laces of my boot.

He carefully tugged the boot free before gently rolling down my sock past my heel.

"How's this?" he asked as his fingers deftly examined my skin.

"Tender," I admitted. "I think I rolled it when I fell."

He stayed focused on my ankle, gently massaging and I stayed at his mercy. He shifted until he was between my legs, then slid off his pack to bring out a first aid kit. He pointed to my knee. "I'll clean this first. Then when we get back to the site, I'll wrap your ankle. You'll need to elevate and ice it."

It was a command and damn if I didn't like this dominating side to him. "Yes, sir," I half-mumbled. We shared another intense look before he ripped the hole in my pants wider, carefully pushing the fabric to the side.

Then he looked up from where he gently held my knee. "Sorry. I can replace these."

I waved him away transfixed at the sight of him staring up at me like that while his fingers tickled the back of my knee.

I swallowed. "It's fine."

He cleaned the wound and I sucked in a breath between my teeth.

"Sorry." He winced. Then, as though without any thought, he lowered his head and let out a low stream of breath onto my knee where he just dabbed it with alcohol. It shot straight to my cock and I had to shift to make room. His eyes went to my crotch.

"Sorry. This is all very sexy and doing things for me," I admitted.

He flushed all the way to the tips of his ears but lifted his eyes to mine as his hands continued to rub my leg. The tips of his fingers tickled the sensitive skin of my upper thighs. I shuddered as he gently smoothed a bandage over the wound.

"Noted," he said with a slight smile pulling at the side of his mouth.

He started to say something else when Ethan shouted down.

"He okay?"

William gave him a thumbs-up and seemed to clear his head. "Think you can make it back up the hill?"

I glanced up the steep terrain noting the saplings about the thickness of poles that dotted the way. "Yeah, thankfully my upper body is strong from the pole dancing lessons," I said.

Did I need to mention the lessons? Probably not. Did I want him to imagine me riding a pole? Absolutely.

He stilled and looked at me. "Pole dancing?" he asked low and rumbling.

"Remember Suzie? She runs a studio and I take lessons from her."

His face remained placid but he swallowed thickly. "Oh." He cleared his throat and said, "Apparently that does things for me too."

"Noted. I'll have to show you sometime."

Heat burned bright in his eyes before dimming a moment later. That's right. There was no "sometime," this would all be over in a few days and he would be gone.

"Let's get you back up," he said.

After he replaced my boot, we made our way slowly back up the side. A few guys helped bring me up the last few feet.

"You okay, Jack?" Ethan asked.

"Yeah, man, you freaked us out," Dominic said.

"No. I'm fine." I let out a sigh. "Only, I don't think I'll be able to take you guys the rest of the way."

"I need to take him back," William said decisively. "His ankle is already swelling."

"Aww, man, but you hyped those falls up so much," Dominic said.

William glared at him.

"But that's fine," he finished, rubbing at his mustache. "We're just glad you're okay," he finished half-heartedly.

"Can't we keep going?" Derek asked.

"I can stay here," I offered, "until you make your way back."

William frowned deeply. "No."

Okay, so much for that idea.

"Sorry, guys, I trust you but this is a chaperoned trip," I explained. "An adult needs to be around at all times."

The guys moaned and sighed.

"Sorry," I said. I really did feel bad. I'd been talking about the falls for weeks. They are beautiful. Seeing the deer had been an amazing experience until I messed it up and I would have liked to give them the falls too.

"I'm eighteen," Ethan offered.

His gaze flicked around the others waiting to be challenged. Only this time, the others didn't mock him. They nodded eagerly.

I ran a hand over my chin. I just wanted to get back and shower this dirt off me. Lord knew what I rolled through making my way down that hill. I trusted them. I looked to William again. He nodded subtly.

"Alright. Here's the deal. Stay on this path to get to the falls and come straight back. No later than five p.m., I want you back. You hear me?"

The guys whooped and punched the air.

William shrugged out of his pack and handed it to Ethan. "Make sure you start heading back by three thirty. There are emergency supplies and bear mace in here. Make sure you apply more sunscreen if you swim."

Ethan nodded solemnly as he adjusted the pack for his much smaller frame.

"I'm trusting y'all with this," I said, looking seriously from face to face.

"Ain't no thing, Jack. We got this," Kyle said.

With that, the guys set off in the direction of the falls. William cleared his throat before stepping close to me. He tentatively looped an arm around my waist and pulled me snug, wrapping my left arm around his shoulders.

"This okay?" he asked and it rumbled through me.

"Yeah," I said and we headed back for camp. Alone.

* * *

William

JACK'S MUSCLES were solid under my hands as I held him tight to me. They flexed with surprising strength as he kept pace. It wasn't surprising though, was it? He was strong enough to lift his entire body up a pole. Images of him working the pole, muscles flexing and legs gripping would forever be seared into my brain. He smelled amazing for day two of camping and for falling down a ravine. This would be a super inappropriate time to sport a chubby. I took a deep breath in through my teeth.

"Think they'll be okay?" he asked.

"Yeah. Ethan seemed up for the challenge."

He nodded. "He seems better. Derek too. It's good to get away."

I nodded. Camping fixed everything.

"Are you okay?" he asked.

I glanced to him, and he smiled at me with his deep dimples and kind eyes. "Am *I* okay?"

"I'm not too heavy, am I?" he clarified.

I hefted him closer, lifting him up off the ground a few inches without losing speed. He was solid muscle but I could easily toss him around and it felt very important to show off that fact. "Nope." I gently lowered him again.

He was able to keep a good pace but I made sure we didn't rush.

"We'd be great at a three-legged race," he said after several minutes of walking in silence.

I grunted. I was having a hard time not thinking dirty thoughts. Especially when his shirt kept riding up and I decided it would just be easier to hold on to him, skin to skin. He was hot to the touch and every exhale tensed his strong core.

"I still can't believe I fell. I feel incredibly stupid. How much would I have to pay you to not tell Ford about this?" he asked.

"One time I fell while I was camping. I cracked my head against a rock and ended up needing stitches," I said. "I hadn't even been doing anything. I just tripped over my gangly teenage feet."

As soon as I shared, I winced. I had been trying to make sure he didn't feel stupid but would he think that I was using this as another opportunity to talk about my friendship with Sanders?

He tensed for a moment and then asked, "Is that where the scar on your chin is from?"

I glared straight ahead. "No. That, uh, was my father."

This time his tensing was much more noticeable. "I'm sorry," he said. "My old man would throw me around too."

I frowned. "He didn't like my stutter. He thought it made me weak. A s-sissy." I gritted my teeth. Just talking about that man brought up so many buried emotions.

I glanced to Jack. His face was twisted in anger.

"He slammed my head against a table. I had permanent nerve damage ever since then. It was after that when William took me in," I explained.

Jack was silent a moment, then finally, he said, "I like the scar. I don't know if that's weird for you, but it reminds me of a sexy pirate or something."

I barked out a laugh.

"How did you end up in the foster system?" I asked.

"You have such a hard time taking compliments." Jack sighed. Heat burned my cheeks. "When I got a little bit bigger, I started fighting back. I was sent to juvie, that's where I met Ford. Our parents, Carol and Joe, took us in. She was his teacher and then she discovered my natural ability for math. She's the reason I got as far as I did. I was lucky to be seen as a child with potential and not another faceless victim of a broken system. Once I was able to pour myself into something challenging and had support, I pulled back on the violence."

"It's hard to imagine you like that," I admitted.

"I'm a much different man that child I used to be. Part of that is intentional. People weren't always accepting of a kid who spoke like he was from the hood," he said.

"You seem so confident in who you are."

"Years of being rejected by everybody, makes you get really good at knowing yourself," he said. "I spent way too much of my life giving value to the opinions of people who wanted nothing more than to see me fail."

I glanced again to Jack. He looked straight ahead, memories passing over his face. So much about this man was a mystery to me and I only had myself to blame. I kept myself so preoccupied with my own shit I didn't even consider the demons he battled.

"You're amazing," I said softly. I couldn't look at him while I said it but he had to know. "You give so much to these guys. You help complete strangers. You're a fucking math professor and you make it all look effort-less. Plus, you're so damn hot it seems criminal."

Jack was quiet for so long I forgot I wasn't supposed to be looking at him. He waited to speak until I stopped to look at him. "Don't forget I ride a pole like no other."

Heat blazed in his eyes.

I stumbled before quickly catching us both.

"We're back," I said about an octave too high.

We stopped just outside the small trail that led back to the tents. We stood arm in arm, staring at each other. I wanted to kiss him so bad.

"Let me wrap your ankle," I said.

"No." He shook his head vehemently. "I'm not doing anything until I shower."

I blinked at him. "You know this is your third shower in twenty-four hours. I'm starting to think it wasn't the guys who insisted on having them."

He shrugged with a strained smile. "Let me get my stuff and take me to the showers."

I wanted him to rest but he seemed determined. At the bathrooms, we carefully stripped him of his ripped pants and tee shirt. I did my best to help him in the shower without ogling his beautiful naked body. I did okay. It was quite a task to keep his weight off one foot while keeping his other knee's bandage from getting too wet. He was large and slippery and in pain. More impressive than all of that was that I managed to keep my clothes on.

"I feel ridiculous," he said as I held his arm and he soaped himself off.

"You just had to have a shower," I teased.

It was little more than a freezing drizzle of water in an open stall. I had locked the door just in case but still wouldn't do anything uncouth. Thankfully, there wasn't much that was sexy about a campsite shower or about him being in pain. Even with all that, if I were to have stripped out of clothes, there was nothing to stop myself from rubbing myself all over him.

"I don't like being dirty," he admitted softly. "It reminds me of a few weeks I lived on the streets."

I bent forward and lightly kissed his damp shoulder. "I'm happy to help you." I purposely let my gaze move down the length of him. "It's not exactly a chore."

He huffed a laugh but his breaths kept getting shorter as he grew quiet. This exertion from the walk back and this shower was getting the best of him. His pain got my horny brain to focus on finishing the task.

He managed to get through the shower and I managed to walk all the way back to the site with him in tow and a boner getting chafed by wet pants.

Back in the tent, I wrangled him inside without causing more injury. Thankfully, the sun had shifted enough for it to be in the shade now, so it was nowhere as hot as it was in the early morning light. By the time he was dressed in his boxers, the skin around his eyes was tight and his dimples nowhere to be seen.

"Here." I handed him some painkillers and a bottle of water. "Take these and lie back so I can wrap this."

He did as told before lying back with a long sigh out. I quickly stripped out of my wet overshirt and pants. He blinked up slowly at me.

"No funny business," I said.

"Hmm," he hummed.

I sat on the ground, delicately bringing his ankle into my lap. It was a little more swollen than before but thankfully not as bad as it could be. Definitely not broken, probably just a little sore for a few days. I checked to make sure the other bandage was still okay before I got to wrapping his ankle.

"Is this okay? Tight but not painful?" I asked.

"Hmm," he hummed again.

When I looked up his eyes were closed and his chest moved up and down. His body was the most beautiful body I'd ever seen. His lean figure was sliced with sharp, defined muscles. A few round scars on his ribs marred otherwise smooth, flawless skin. He had the slightest happy trail starting just below his belly button and dipped into his boxers, teasing me. His cock twitched and I looked up to find him watching. The action of pulling his head up emphasized a tight six-pack.

"No funny business," he repeated.

"Can you blame a guy?" I mumbled with a smile.

He chuckled and relaxed back. I cracked an ice pack to active it and laid it gently on his ankle. I grabbed an extra blanket, rolling it up to prop up his leg. I took my time with every bit of activity, reluctant to end this free access to touching him.

"I've been thinking"—his words were slurred with sleep—"I'm going to start calling you Skip too."

I stilled, flicking him a glance.

"Oh?" I said.

"The more I think about it, the more I think it's perfect for you."

Despite all that we'd shared, knowing he was one of the kindest people I'd ever met, my stomach still tightened in fear.

He blinked slowly as I scooted around to sit on my own sleeping bag. I didn't know what to say. The fact was, I'd spoken more this week and with more confidence than I think I ever had. Something about being around him empowered me. Now, I felt a little queasy.

"Yup," he said dopily, half asleep. "The first time I saw you at the drag show, my heart *skipped*."

I was unmoving, hardly able to process what I just heard. He went on.

"Then when I saw you again at Genie's, my heart *skipped* again. Hearing you talk to the guys. Watching you work with your hands." His eyes were closed and he sighed. My chest heaved up and down. "Whenever I'm around you my heart skips. See, Skip. It's perfect for you."

Chills broke out over my skin. Emotion made my throat so tight, I almost couldn't breathe. Moisture stung my eyes.

I lay down on the sleeping bag next to him, propped up on one elbow. "Jack," I choked out his name.

He fluttered his eyes open to look at me.

"I—" I tried to speak but nothing could suffice.

He shook his head slowly once.

I lowered my head to him, my whole body shaking though I wasn't sure why. I kissed him softly on the lips.

He moaned as he opened to my tongue. We kissed softly, slowly, sweetly. For a long time, we kissed like there was nothing else in the world.

Eventually he dropped back with a sigh. I had to let him sleep. I pulled him into my arms where he relaxed instantly. I kissed the top of his head as he exhaled a contented sigh. He was sound asleep in moments. My heart hammered away in my chest.

My brain swirled with overwhelming emotion. I shouldn't feel this much so soon. I shouldn't feel like the ground was shifting underneath me. I shouldn't feel like the whole world had just turned upside down.

I must have fallen asleep burying myself in shouldn'ts.

The next thing I knew I was jolted out of sleep. The light was much dimmer. My heart clawed with panic but I couldn't understand why.

I grabbed my watch and looked at the time. It was after 7 p.m. and the campsite was silent.

"Oh my God." I sat up so quickly Jack shook awake.

"What's wrong?" he mumbled with sleep.

"The guys." I scrambled to pull on pants and a shirt. "They aren't back."

CHAPTER 12

SKIP

I crashed out of the tent and toward the trail. I wasn't fully awake or thinking. I just knew I had to get to the guys and nothing else mattered.

I stopped short.

They were there. I did a quick head count. All ten of them were there.

I sagged with my hands on my knees.

"Yo, Brawny Man awakens," someone shouted.

I was too busy catching my breath to see who. I hoped Ethan hadn't seen the look of absolute fear on my face and think I didn't trust him. I had assumed the worst.

When I finally gathered my breath, my other senses started working. The fire crackled loudly and the smell of cooking meat and potatoes wafted through the air.

"You guys started dinner?" Jack asked, his eyebrows up in surprise and his dimples deep.

He had used a stick to hobble over next to me.

"Yeah," Ethan said, standing up from where he prodded the fire. He dusted off his hands. "We wanted to make sure we got started before it got too late."

"I didn't hear you guys," I mumbled.

"We heard you snoring and didn't want to wake you," he said.

"We thought it was an avalanche at first," Kyle said.

"You should probably see a doctor about that," Dominic added.

I huffed a laugh too relieved to feel anything else but joy.

"You okay, Brawny Man?" Ethan asked.

"Yeah, of course." I straightened to come help get plates and forks ready. "How were the falls?"

They all spoke at once.

"Amazing."

"Religious."

"Life changing."

"They were alright," that from Derek who shot a shy glance to Ethan.

Ethan flushed and went back to the fire.

I brought Jack to a chair and forced him to sit with his foot up on a stump. He gave me a grumpy look but did as I ordered.

"Thanks, Skip," he said quietly.

I shot my gaze to his, as my heart went crazy. I wasn't sure that he would remember that whole half-asleep conversation. I wasn't sure if I had dreamt it.

It was hard to not keep shooting him secret glances as the night went on. Somehow, every time I did, he caught me and smiled easily. And every time he did, I felt the earth shift a little more. I felt my self-control slip a little more.

At dinner, I pulled my chair up next to Ethan. We sat a little to the side so I could talk to him without the others hearing.

"Thanks for today," I said to him.

He lifted his chin and shrugged. "No big deal."

"It is a big deal," I said with emphasis.

He held my gaze and nodded. I wondered if he realized this was so similar and so far from our first conversation.

"How'd it go?" I asked gesturing to the rest of the group.

"Good. They got a little crazy in the water but they had fun," he said.

I could already see that he was differentiating himself from the rest of the group. His gaze flicked to Derek. He and Jack spoke quietly a little bit away, also off to the side. Jack was speaking with low intensity and Derek frowned at the ground with arms crossed.

"This is my last trip," Ethan said.

I brought my focus back to him. His face was solemn.

"Because you're eighteen now?"

He nodded. "I was thinking." He cleared his throat and sat up straighter. "Maybe I could still hang around. Maybe volunteer. Jack got me an apprenticeship with an electrician, but maybe ..."

"I think that would be great. You're a natural leader. I bet Jack and Ford would love all the help they could get."

He nodded, sucking in his lips, hiding a smile.

He grabbed a stick and I handed him the knife I'd been using to whittle. I showed him how to angle the blade and let him try.

"You gonna come around more too?" he asked and I swore he sent a quick, knowing glance to Jack.

"I-I—" I swallowed after almost biting my lip again. "I live in Denver," I settled on.

"That's not what I asked," he said with his old familiar attitude.

I shot him a look and he shrugged.

We sat quietly and I stared at the fire. Being here was making me want things I couldn't want. But why not? Maybe I could talk to Sanders about pulling out of OTB. Maybe I could come back ... The thought of never seeing these kids again tightened my chest and the thought of never seeing Jack again made me feel like I would never breathe again.

When had that happened? When did he become more important than oxygen?

With another glance, I checked in on Derek and Jack who still talked in low voices. Jack had his hand on Derek's shoulder, head lowered to impress something important on him. Derek had his hand over his eyes, hood up as always, shoulders shaking slightly.

Ethan noticed me watching them. He frowned.

He cleared his throat. "That stuff with Derek's twin, Chloe. That was a dick move."

"Yeah," I said. "Know better. Do better."

"I promise I'm not leading her on." He shifted in his chair. "Derek and I are, uh— We hook up sometimes but she doesn't know."

I nodded, careful not to give any look that might get him to stop talking.

"I go over there a lot. Their dad doesn't seem to fuck with them as much if someone else is there."

My fists flexed and I glared at the fire. I would need to talk to Jack about this.

"I think she might think it's in part for her. I can be a bit of a flirt," he admitted.

I raised an eyebrow. I knew the type. It was the first time I had thought of Sanders in a while.

"As soon as they're eighteen, we're all gonna move in together. And I'm gonna make sure that ass-wipe never fucks with him again." His voice got tight. "Derek purposely gets his dad riled up so that he won't go after Chloe." He cut off and turned his head away with a sniff.

It took a minute before I could speak. What could I even say? Was there anything I could do?

I focused instead on something I might be able to actually help with. "You have to talk to her. Chloe. Before you all move in together. Or that's going to blow up in your face. Epically."

"Yeah, I know." Ethan sighed deeply.

We both looked to Jack and Derek. Derek stood up and rolled his shoulders. He shot a look to Ethan before turning and walking into the woods.

Ethan stood up a second later. "You should think about it. Visiting," he said. "It would be cool to do this again."

He walked away into the direction of the trees without waiting for a response. A moment later, Jack sat in the chair Ethan just left.

"Derek okay?" I asked.

Jack's mouth was a tight line. He shook his head. "I want to murder that asshole sperm donor of his."

I was shocked at the vehemence in his voice. His fists were balled and he stared into the fire, the light dancing in his tortured eyes.

"Me too. What can we do?"

He shook his head. "Ford and I have called Tennessee's Department of Children's Services many times. I'm close to stepping in."

I understood his desire. Even I wanted to step in. Eliminate the problem. But rationally, we had to think. "Would that put Triple F at risk?"

"That's the only thing that's stopped me. There are too many other kids that need it." He shook his head. "This is the part I hate, man. This fucking feeling of helplessness. The system is in place to help but fuck if it doesn't seem like it's making things worse."

"Ethan said they'll all be eighteen and living together soon," I offered.

"Yeah, end of August; I'm hoping sooner. But how will they afford it? I don't know if any of them even have a job. Ethan will be okay but he won't make real money as an electrician for a few years."

"Kids are resilient. They'll figure it out. They aren't alone. They have you." I almost said they have me too. But they didn't, did they? I would have to leave.

Jack swallowed and ran a hand over his short-cropped hair. "I just hate feeling like there's nothing I can do."

"I know," I whispered.

That night Jack and I went to bed at the same time. We changed in silence. He unzipped the sleeping bags making a bottom blanket and top blanket for us to share. When I slid in, he curled into me, laying his head on my chest. We fit perfectly together. He must have heard the way my heart beat frantically for him.

I couldn't find the words for all the complicated mashup of feelings that warred inside me. For the first time in a long time, I had no idea what was coming next. I had no idea what I wanted. It had been so long since I even considered it.

All I could hope was that Sanders hadn't done anything crazy while I was gone. We had things that we needed to figure out. We had a business.

"Skip?" he whispered and despite my worries I smiled.

I turned to him in the dark. Our mouths found each other. We kissed silently for a long time. We kissed until we knew we had to stop or risk doing something unprofessional.

Much later we fell asleep and I decided that whatever came next would have to involve Jack in some way.

CHAPTER 13

JACK

The bus arrived early the next morning. Skip and I had packed up as much as we could while we let the guys sleep.

Skip.

After a night of slow kisses and quiet sighs, we couldn't seem to stop smiling at each other. Something had shifted between us. Something that I hoped would lead to more. He hadn't mentioned Denver or Sanders for some time. Of course he had a whole life he needed to get back to but maybe a future for us and his other life didn't have to be mutually exclusive.

Eventually, we roused the guys and got the bus loaded. My ankle felt loads better but Skip still doted on me hand and foot, and who was I to stop him? Almost immediately upon loading the bus and hitting the road, the guys fell asleep.

Skip and I held hands in the front seat. There was no need to come up with a pretense of reasons to sit next to each other this time.

I glanced up to him and smiled. I lowered my head to his shoulder.

"I probably should have showered. I can smell myself," Skip said.

I turned to inhale him deeply. "I think you smell good. Very manly."

He flushed and I would never tire of finding ways to make him blush. I wished I could kiss him the whole drive back to Green Valley but that probably wouldn't be great for Triple F.

The drive felt so much faster on the return that it seemed to defy the laws of physics. Soon the familiar exit to Green Valley was upon us.

"I'm not ready for this trip to end," Skip said.

I sat up and squeezed his hand tighter. "Me neither."

He was quiet again, reminding me of when we first met. Reminding me how far we've come in just a few short days. I wasn't ready to let this go, whatever it was.

"I think we need to talk about the elephant in the room," I said, tentatively. Despite myself, despite the incredible few days we shared, my palms began to sweat.

He looked up at me, his brows furrowed. He worried the numb part of his lip, still a little red. I wanted to kiss and suck on it.

"What?" he asked.

"What's next?" I asked, hopeful and terrified.

He ran his free hand over his beard. "I don't know. I have to go back to Denver. The team needs to know what's going on."

It wasn't a door slammed in my face. I let out a slow breath. I licked my dry lips. "Definitely. And then maybe you can come visit? Or I can come to Denver," I added quickly.

He smiled at our clasped hands. "Absolutely. Sanders wouldn't mind you staying with us."

I swallowed with effort. "You and Sanders live together?"

"Yeah. We always have."

I kept my breath steady. "I think we need to talk about him. Sanders."

He tensed. "Sanders?"

"Listen. I see how you look at him. I hear how you talk about him. I understand that you have a lot of history that I can never understand, but." I cleared my throat. My heart was pounding. But there was no going back. This had to all be laid out there. "I'm not going to let myself fall for someone who's already in love with someone else."

There. I had said it. I had admitted my feelings and my fears.

Skip dropped my hand. "I am *not* in love with him," he hissed and looked around like anybody could even hear us.

I sat stock-still. I had confessed I was falling for him and he completely glazed over that; instead, as always, focusing on Sanders. I scoffed, shaking my head. I had really been so stupid.

"Jesus, how could you even say that?" he said. "We're basically b-b. We're best friends."

The more he denied it, the colder my limbs went. "Brothers. You can't even say it. Ford and I are like brothers. I have never, ever, looked at him in any other way. Can you say that?"

He snubbed his hands through his dirty hair, making it even more wild. "This is ridiculous. I don't have to defend myself to you."

"I just thought we should talk about things." I kept my voice calm but inside I knew the truth.

He was so far in denial. It was worse than I thought.

"There's nothing to talk about," he said evenly.

"You followed him to Green Valley."

"He's hurting. He needs me. His father just died." He tossed a hand out.

"You continue to put your dreams on hold for his," I said flatly.

His gaze shuttered. He had told me that hoping I'd forget, but I hadn't. His nostrils were flared and he panted in anger. Maybe I had gone too far.

"You don't know anything."

"You're wrong," I snapped. "I've been here before. Freshman year of college I made the absolutely terrible mistake to fall for a TA. He strung me along, as a backup for years. He would come to me with all these complaints about his husband. That's my regret that I have to live with," I said when his eyebrows shot up to the news that I had been with a married person. I went on, "He told me over and over he would leave his partner for me. I was a fool but I believed him. I thought it was real love." I was ashamed at the hurt that still came out sharing this part of my past. The shame and the humiliation. "I thought we were in a relationship but I was nothing but a booty call used to make his husband jealous. For years. In the end it wasn't even a choice for him. I was nothing."

He frowned. "I'm sorry, Jack. I'm so sorry. That was so fucked up of him."

I waited for the "but" I felt coming. I hardened myself against him. I mustered all the anger I could to cover the pain that was ripping through me.

"But this isn't like that. I am not in love with Sanders."

I huffed. "It looks like it where I'm standing."

"So what? You want me to stop talking to my best friend on the planet, the person I've known the longest, just to prove that I like you? Are you that petty?"

I felt like I'd been slapped. I lowered my voice. We were almost to the Lodge and the guys were starting to rouse. "I would never make you choose. That's the difference," I hissed. "When does Sanders ever consider you when he makes a choice?"

His nostrils flared and he swallowed.

"That's what I thought. I'm not asking you to choose me, Skip. I'm asking you to choose yourself for once and see what happens."

"You don't understand. Sanders loves me. We are there for each other."

"Okay." I lifted one shoulder and dropped it. "I hope that's true."

The bus rolled to a stop. The driver barely got the door opened in time before he was down the stairs.

I jogged after him. Like a damn fool.

He was already halfway across the lobby. He was headed right to Sanders. I tossed my hands out and shook my head with a laugh. Of course he was. Straight to him.

"Really?" I said to myself.

Sanders had his attention now. I was already forgotten.

I got back on the bus and told my stupid heart to shut up. I had warned it this would happen. I had told it and my heart ignored me. I told myself it was different this time. That I would be the one that he chose. I was so painfully wrong.

I wasn't letting myself forget this feeling ever again.

* * *

THE RAIN CRASHED against the windows, thunder shaking the frames. I tossed onto my side.

After midnight and I was wired. Not a word from Skip. Nothing. I was forgotten about. No matter how I told myself to stop thinking about him, he was all I could see when my eyes drifted closed. So many beautiful images of him and they wouldn't leave me alone. It was no longer safe to shut my eyes.

My doorbell rang.

I balled my fists, willing myself to be hallucinating.

The doorbell rang again.

"Don't do it," I told myself. "Please don't do it."

A crash of thunder shook the house even harder. I couldn't leave him out there in this storm.

"Fuck," I swore.

I threw back the blankets and stomped toward the front door, not bothering to put on any more clothes. Ford and Suzie were still gone.

I knew who I'd find.

Skip stood soaking wet, head bowed when I opened the door. His nickname painfully prophetic as he looked up, blinking rapidly as water poured down his face.

"I couldn't leave like this. W-w-without—" It wasn't his stutter that caused him to trip over his words. His blue lips trembled and his whole body convulsed with shivers.

"Get in here."

I pulled him inside to the foyer. My heart and brain battling like never before. I was so happy to see him but only delaying the inevitable. Only pushing the sword deeper into my heart, so that when it was removed, I'd likely bleed out.

And yet, he was here for now.

I tugged off his flimsy soaked-through coat. He helped me slide his shirt up and off through convulses of shivers. I dropped to my knees to remove his sodden boots, wincing a little at the still fresh scratch on my knee but not caring. His jeans required more tugging and he wobbled pitifully as I managed to tug them down over his massive thighs. His whole damp body was covered in goose bumps. His little brown nipples pebbled as he shivered, arms crossed in front of him. For such an imposingly large man, he'd never seemed smaller or more unsure.

I stepped forward and kissed him lightly on the cheek. He sighed and leaned slightly into me. His skin was icy and clammy where it pressed against my chest and arms.

"Come on," I said before leading him to the bathroom.

I turned the shower all the way up and soon the bathroom was filled with steam. He stepped into the shower, shaking even harder now. He looked at me with mournful eyes but I left to drop a towel on the patch of water by the door and toss his clothes in the dryer.

Outside the threshold of the bathroom, I gripped the handle knowing whatever I did next would hurt. But how could I not take what I could get? I was setting myself up for hurt, but he was *here* just for tonight.

I took a deep breath in and stepped into the steaming bathroom. I stripped off my drawers and stepped into the shower. His head was down, the water flattening his hair. His head jerked up in surprise when he sensed my presence behind him.

"I—"

I cut him off with my mouth. I kissed him so hard he fell back against the wall with a moan of relief like I'd never heard. I kissed him harder than ever, holding nothing back. *This is what could have been yours*, I seemed to tell him as I sucked his tongue and licked his neck. *This is how it could have been.* He kissed me back just as hard, fingers gripping my shoulders so hard they seemed to say, *You're not going anywhere now.*

His shivers were long gone. His skin burned because the fire between us was strong as ever. We were both rock hard in seconds. We held each other so tight our slick cocks rutted against each other as desperate as our mouths.

"Jack," he gasped as I wrapped my hand around his dick.

Fuck he was so hard. I kissed his strong neck and shoulders, nuzzling his hairy chest, all the while stroking him.

I turned him to face the water as I lathered my hands up with soap. I worked it all over his strong back and shoulders, all the way down his arms to his hands. He grabbed mine to wrap my arms around him. He turned his head to kiss me deeply. The soap on his back blended onto my skin, making me as slippery as him. I thrust myself against his ass, breaking our kiss to gasp in a breath. I slicked my fingers and lowered them to tease him. He groaned, head back, beautiful strong neck being splattered with water. The rich scent of him clung to the humidity in the air, driving me mad. My fingers probed him gently, first one finger, then another to open him to me.

"Oh God," he cried out as I worked him. "I'm too close."

"Not yet," I demanded and removed my fingers. "I'm supposed to have you begging for it."

He turned to me, eyes burning, color high on his cheeks. "It won't take much."

We finished washing each other in a series of gasps and sliding limbs broken up with kisses. We were rushing to finish with this, knowing we didn't want our first and only time to be in a shower, no better than a gym hookup. Or at least that's what I thought.

I turned off the shower. I gently toweled him off, emotions made me quiet, unable to say much besides the occasional command. Now I know how he felt. How everything I felt was too big, too important to ruin with misspoken good intentions. Best to let my body do the talking tonight.

He dried me with equal reverence, taking care of my knee and ankle. His gaze held something I refused to see. If I saw pity there, I wouldn't be able to go through with this. If I saw something more, my heart wouldn't be able to take it. I wanted this night at least. I *needed* this and then I would let him go.

Dried and back in my bed, he lay back against my duvet and pillows like the hulking god that he was. With hands clasped behind his head, and legs sprawled, his muscular frame peppered with dark, coarse hair, his massive hard cock lying against the hard planes of his abdomen, he was truly a sight.

I took a mental picture despite myself. *In* spite of myself because I knew I would never forget this image. I could never make him love me. I would never want to make him do so if his heart was with someone else. I wouldn't come between a relationship decades old. But I also would never forget this moment.

He beckoned me with his familiar half smile and the lick of his lips. I pushed all other thoughts aside. I turned the lights down and turned on some soft music. I crawled to him and straddled him. He lifted to kiss me and I met him halfway, feeling his muscles flex under me. I closed my eyes and lost myself to the kiss.

We kissed and kissed, tongues colliding, taking turns sucking each other's lips, until the heat became too much between us. We were slick where we thrust against each other. I had never wanted anybody this bad.

I couldn't make him love me. I couldn't make him stay in Tennessee. But we could have tonight. And when he left, I would try to stay standing.

I kissed my way down his body. So warm. So strong. So fucking good.

I took him into my mouth giving instinctually what I knew he needed. I teased and sucked and kissed all around him. I licked and flicked my tongue against his inner thighs. He swore, sweaty and panting against the pillows.

"I want to be inside you," I said.

He fisted the blanket, head thrown back, teeth bared. "God, yes."

"You want me to fuck you?" I asked and licked the area behind his balls until he couldn't sit still. I went higher yet.

"Fuck me. Please."

I put his knees on my shoulders and he lifted his hips for me as I continued to tongue him and make him ready. He groaned and stroked himself. The blanket was damp where my own hard dick thrust impatiently.

Only I could bring him to this point. Only I could make him feel this good. There were only two people in this bed. His sweaty legs slid off me as I reached for the bottle of lube and a condom. I slicked my fingers before testing him. He spread even wider for me. When I looked up at him, he stared down at me where I worked between his legs.

"Jack," he gasped out my name. "I need you now."

I worked another finger in. Not relenting to his demands quite yet even though my balls were painful with the need to release.

"I'm begging you," he ground out.

I grinned up at him. "Well, okay, then."

Making my way up, I kissed his thighs and abdomen. My tongue swirled his nipples as his hands impatiently tugged me higher up his body. When our mouths met again, he held me close and lifted his knees as I shifted. I slid in and we groaned in unison.

I shook my head as I slowly moved, making more room for myself. It was too good. He was too good.

"So good," he slurred in agreement and I realized I had been chanting those words out loud. "It's never felt like this."

I thought I had been thinking out loud again but that sentiment was his. Sweat collected on me as I fought to maintain control. Electricity shot down my spine and collected in my balls. I couldn't hold on much longer.

"Jack," he said.

I buried my face into his neck as I thrust into him. He was hard as steel, rubbing his slickness against my stomach. I was so close already. He felt too tight and perfect.

"Jack," he repeated until I lifted to look at him. His gaze flicked between my own, a flash of worry in his gaze. He shook as he lifted to kiss me briefly. "Look at me while you're making me feel this good."

I swallowed and lifted onto shaking arms to do just that. His gaze searched mine, looking for something. I thrust even deeper, watching him burn for me.

"You feel amazing," he said. "So fucking good."

Who'd have thought of the two of us, he'd be the more vocal one during sex.

My heart hammered out of control. I dropped my forehead to his, searching his eyes. My whole body shook. I couldn't do this. I couldn't look at him and do this. I felt too much. He opened his mouth to speak but I kissed him again. I closed my eyes against the pain breaking my heart. It couldn't be hurting this bad. It was too soon for this to hurt so fucking bad while feeling so good. So right. We fit so perfect together.

I rocked my hips as our tongues battled each other. He broke the kiss to groan out a moment later. Wet heat splashed my stomach and chest. It was too much.

"Fuck," I cried out before I followed him a second later. A release that seemed to go on and on. I collapsed on to him, sweaty but not caring as I slid off to the side. I pulled off the condom, tied it off and tossed it into the trash.

It was several minutes before either one of us could breathe normally. Eventually I managed to get out of bed to get a towel to clean us off. With every passing second the heat dissipated into cold regret. I felt way too much. This was going to hurt way more than my last heartbreak. It already hurt more.

I needed to tell him to leave now. I should have never opened that door to him. When was I going to learn?

When he pulled me onto his chest, I went like the damn fool I was. His heart beat strongly beneath my ear. I closed my eyes and inhaled him, luxuriating in the sense of security at his presence.

I wouldn't let myself fall asleep. I would draw the line there.

"This house is beautiful. I can't wait to see it in the daylight."

I squeezed my eyes tighter and took a deep breath in and out. "It's a historic home," I said.

Any other mood, any other day I would have teased him with the knowledge that there was a pole in the basement. But I couldn't find any light in the darkness of my thoughts. I knew I was stiff in his arms. He must sense something was wrong.

Was he still mad at me for my accusations on the bus? Why did he come here tonight? What were we even doing? I thought this would be okay. I thought once we did this, maybe I would feel at least I'd gotten something out of it. I had been lying to myself. All I felt now was an aching pit of loneliness and regret.

He didn't respond to my last comment. And I didn't respond to him seeing the house during the day. I wouldn't even let my mind go there. No topic felt safe when this was coming to an end in minutes. I would never let myself have such ridiculous daydreams like seeing him cooking in my kitchen or folding towels to put away in the closet. Such silly stupid imaginations they would be anyway.

"My flight is at noon," he said and it was just what I needed to refocus. He was leaving. When would I get it through my head?

When I couldn't find words, he went on.

"Sanders went back already. He just left without telling me. He says the Lodge wants to partner with OTB. He said he was moving here. Without talking to me. He didn't even ask—"

With every word he spoke, the pressure built under my skull until I felt like I would burst. I shot out of bed. I couldn't take a moment more of this.

"No." My head shook back and forth as I pulled on pants.

"What?" He sat up, eyes wide.

"Get out," I growled.

"What?" he asked in absolute shock.

"I'm not doing this again," I said holding his gaze.

My heart was breaking. I could actually feel the walls crumbling in on themselves. I couldn't take it. I forced ice into it. I ran to the dryer to grab his clothes. I tossed them at him when I returned. He was still standing there dumbfounded.

"Doing what?" William got up and put his pants on, his own voice rising in anger.

"I'm not going to fuck you and then listen to you vent all about someone else. You need to leave."

His head shook back and forth, his face was twisting as I spoke.

"Fucking? That's what that was?" He gestured to the bed.

"I've spent enough of my life being treated like shit. I'm not doing this anymore."

"I never meant to make you feel that way. Jack, I—" The look in his eyes terrified me.

"Don't finish that sentence," I ground out the words, jaw clenched. "Not until you're absolutely sure you know what you're saying."

His mouth closed slowly. Just like I thought.

"I'm not messing around with all that, man. You need to figure your shit out. I don't want to be runner-up." I started to the door and he stomped after me.

"It's not like that."

"It's not? To me it looks like you follow him around everywhere he goes. Cleaning up his mistakes. Waiting for him to need you. You enable him. He's never going to grow up when you are always there."

"S-s-s." He took a deep breath in and I turned to the door to unlock it. "He just needs a little patience. He's having a hard time."

"Yeah, you keep saying that. What about you? What about me? We all go through shit. We figure out how to heal from it and we grow up and move on. We don't bring down the people we love in the wake of our bad choices."

William's face morphed into anger. "It must be nice to have it all figured out."

"Don't fucking do that. Don't presume to know anything about the shit I deal with. You hardly know anything about me because you spend all your time thinking about him."

He shoved on his jacket. "This was a mistake to come here."

"No fucking kidding."

He stood at the door, his chest heaving up and down. "To think I—"

"Just stop." I held up a hand.

He shook his head, his cheeks ruddy and his hair disheveled.

"Goodbye, Jack," he said.

I swallowed and held his gaze. "Goodbye, William."

His hurt anger was the last thing I saw before I shut and locked the door behind him. My hands shook as I slid the chain in.

I was alone in a big house all by myself. Just like I would be from now on.

I let myself do the one thing I promised myself I never would do again. I fell in love with someone who loved someone else.

CHAPTER 14

SKIP

I chose him. I went to him. I went to what I wanted and he pushed me away. I was mad at Jack for pushing me away without even talking to me. I was mad at Sanders for acting reckless once again. But more than anyone, I was furious with myself for being so fucking clueless.

One thing was clear now. More clear than anything else. Jack was wrong. I wasn't in love with Sanders. Maybe, I had allowed myself to think that what I felt was romantic love on some subconscious level, but it never was. A few nights with Jack and I fully understood that nothing could be remotely close to what I felt for him. Sanders was my best friend and I would always care about him.

But this chapter of our lives was over. My mind was made up and the choice was clear.

It was always going to be Jack. From the first moment I found him holding me in that alley. On some level I understood. Jack who last looked at me with such hurt and rejection. I couldn't think about him without my stomach cramping with regret.

"Heya, hot stuff." A voice broke me from my thoughts.

"You've got to be kidding me," I said.

I stood outside the Lodge in the early morning exhausted from not having slept in almost twenty-four hours. I leaned toward the ride that had arrived to take me to the airport. Sanders had taken the rental when he stormed out of here.

"Headed to the airport?" Gretchen LaRoe asked innocently.

"Are you the only driver in this whole town?"

"The best one." She winked.

I put my stuff in the back and fought the ever-present lump in my throat as I got in the passenger seat.

"Heading back already? Feels like you just got here," she said once I was settled.

I glared out the window.

"So Sanders is gone too?" she asked innocently enough.

I guessed whatever weirdness went on between her and Roxy meant they were still not talking. I grunted.

"And, uh, Roxy? How does she seem?"

I softened at the obvious concern in her voice for her friend. I had spent last night talking to Roxy. Before I went to Jack's. She told me that I deserved better.

I had better.

I lost better.

"She's not great. Another person lost in the wake of Sanders," I mumbled.

Her fingers tapped the steering wheel. "You seem grumpier than normal."

I flicked an annoyed glance to her.

"How'd the trip with Jack go? He hasn't responded to my texts."

I grunted.

"Oh shit. Maybe Mercury is in retrograde or something. Roxy still isn't talking to me either."

I sighed loudly, hoping to deflect her from delving into her own issues. My head was throbbing and I needed to think things through.

"I think she's lying to herself," she went on like I wasn't obviously annoyed. "She is in love with Sanders but she let him leave."

"He has a life in Denver. He can't just drop everything to be here," I practically growled.

"Why not?"

I didn't let her bait me again.

"People can change their plans. People change their plans all the time." She continued to talk and I tried my hardest to tune her out. She went on and on about people living in fear of the only real thing they experienced. I tried so hard to ignore her but her anxiety at my silence only made her talk more.

"I was in love once." The sudden shift in her tone caused me to tune back in fully. "I thought my life ended when I lost him. I really thought it was the end of the world. I would look around and wonder how people could keep going on like nothing happened."

"I-I'm sorry," I said.

"I'm just telling you this because … Okay, so fine. Maybe I stick my nose in other people's business. But I *know* love. I know it. And when I see it in other people, I can't stop myself. It's just that—" She stopped talking and sniffled uncharacteristically. When she started again, her voice was lowered. "If you have that sort of opportunity, you have to do whatever you can to hold on to it. Far as I can tell, that's the whole point."

"Point?"

"Of everything."

I sighed and leaned my head back, closing my eyes. If I just hadn't shared that night with Jack, I would have thought she sounded insane, but something shifted. I was changed and for the first time in so long I felt like I wanted more than I had.

"I worry that Roxy is trying to prove something by pushing him away," she said. "I just can't figure out what. I worry that she isn't living life for herself, always putting other people's opinions first. She doesn't even know what she wants."

I cleared my throat and shifted. How could she know her words felt so pointed?

She went on, "I'm not getting involved with Jack and you. But you do remind me of Roxy." I flicked a look to her. "In your head a lot," she clarified. "But Roxy seems to live for other people and that only leads to hurt feelings and resentment. She has to live for herself. I just want her to be happy. That's all anybody wants for the ones they love."

It clicked for me in that moment. What felt to me as a sense of obligation to Sanders and his father had corrupted us from the inside out. We were friends first. He continued to live as though that was the case, selfishly maybe, but for himself knowing I'd support him no matter what. He believed in our love. Whereas I treated him like a savior but a fragile one that needed my saving. I didn't believe that he would love me if I were just honest. When we lost William, I thought I had to cling tighter to him. He was the only family I had. His love was hurting me.

No more.

"I think you should call Roxy," I said.

Gretchen raised an eyebrow.

"I'm sure she wants to talk to you too. She misses you," I added.

Gretchen and I talked about Green Valley the rest of the ride. It was impossible not to like her. When she showed her true self, there was no way not to. I wished she would find her own happy ending. Not one that involved making other people happy. She deserved to find another true love and I wished that for her.

When I got back to Denver, things would change. From now on, I lived for myself and I would trust that Sanders would want that for me.

* * *

Jack

THE GREENS of the summer faded into the oranges and reds of fall. I worked. I volunteered with Triple F and I pushed thoughts of Skip aside. I told myself I had imagined the feelings and built them up. I wasn't used to lying to myself so much. I helped Suzie and Ford pack. She, of course, had loved the house. They told me they would stay as long as I needed them to until I found a roommate, but I knew I had to sell it. It was a lot of house for just one person and the thought of living here alone was too painful.

I lay facedown in the bed and inhaled. There was none of his scent left that I could discern. Just me. I pulled up the photo I had taken of us on the bus. Him sleeping on my shoulder. Lord, I was a fool.

"Hey, it's laundry day," Ford said from the door.

I sighed without looking up. "Yeah. I know."

"I can't help but notice this is now the third straight laundry day you have skipped washing those sheets."

I turned my head to him. "Point being?"

"Point being?" He curled his nose in distaste. "This isn't like you. I'm really starting to worry. Dirty sheets, man."

I sighed and sat up. "No reason to worry." I started to pull up one corner of this fitted sheet, but when it was too much effort, I groaned and fell face-first into my pillow.

Ford moved to the chaise in the corner. "You were right to tell him he needs to figure his shit out."

"But?" I mumbled through the pillow.

"*And*," he said pointedly. "You act like you did it to protect yourself from getting hurt again."

I rolled onto my back. "That's exactly what I did."

"No." He flicked a piece of lint off his pants haughtily.

I sat up. "No?"

"You already got hurt. You *are* hurt." He pointed to the bed to prove his point. "Now you're protecting your pride."

I didn't like where this was going.

"What's-his-face fucked with you and ever since then I've seen you push away every single person who tried to get close to you. Not everyone is him," he said.

"You know his name."

"I don't want to say it. He isn't worth the mention. But this business with Skip. I'm just worried you gave up before you even tried."

"It's been over two months of silence," I said.

"Did you reach out to him?" he asked.

He knew I hadn't.

"I know that you both are working on yourselves but nothing says you can't figure your shit out together. Suzie and I are still learning about each other."

"I know. I hear the fights."

"Not fights. Communicating. We have to be together to do that. We both have to be putting in the effort. Weren't you the one that mentioned something similar to me when I pushed her away?"

I rubbed at my forehead. Had I pushed Skip away too fast? He had shown up that night. He came to me, and before I even reached for him, I knew I would send him away. I knew I felt way too much for him. I groaned and leaned back, head against the headboard.

"I know. But you made me this way. So really you only have yourself to blame," Ford said.

"Yeah, yeah."

"It just sucks that I can't talk about you when I see him."

I slowly turned my head back to him. "What do you mean?"

"Well, like the last trip with Triple F, I wanted to see how he was but I didn't want him to feel weird." Ford would not look at me. Instead he fidgeted with the cuff of his pants.

"You're fucking with me," I said. "He's been out here?"

"At least three times."

I stood up and began to pace. "And you didn't think to mention this before now?"

Ford opened his mouth, then closed it with a frown. "I thought I had."

"Uhm, no. I would definitely remember that. How did Suzie not tell me?"

"Yeah, I don't know." Ford scratched at his beard. "Especially since he's hung out with Roxy a few times on his trips back here. I think they're both mourning the loss of Sanders."

"Wait, what?" I stopped and my stomach dropped. What the hell had I missed?

"Well, no not like that," Ford corrected quickly. "He has fallen off the map too. Getting his life in order."

"Jesus, Ford. Sometimes you really need to think before you speak."

"That's all I do. Apparently so well I often forget to speak."

I glared at my best friend. He wasn't fooling me.

"He asked me not to mention his trips yet," he said on a sigh.

"Why?" I asked.

Ford shrugged.

"So why are you telling me now?" I asked on a tight swallow.

Ford gestured to the bed. "Your sheets, man. I can't take it anymore."

I rolled my eyes. "Oh come on."

"I think he's trying to figure some things out before he talks to you. Today, he said he was going to call you."

"He's here?"

Ford looked up and to the side. "No?" he said without looking at me.

"You really are a terrible liar."

My phone buzzed and my heart leaped into my throat. There was no way … it couldn't be him. But when I read the text, that same heart dropped into my stomach.

"What is it?" Ford asked, reading me.

"Ethan texted me. Derek is in trouble."

CHAPTER 15

SKIP

I burst into the beaten-down house and found him standing in front of the fridge with a beer can pressed to his mouth. I stomped into the kitchen, the old wood floors creaking with every clomp of my boots. He flicked a glance to me before he cracked open the can and started chugging. If he was surprised to have a complete stranger bust into his home, he made absolutely no show.

"Where is he?" I asked in a low voice.

He was a few inches shorter than me but he beat me in girth. A tee shirt that may have been white at some point was yellow and stained and spread tight over an enormous beer belly. He wobbled unsteadily on his feet as he turned to me.

"And who the fuck are you?" he asked with slow blinks.

With him facing me, I could see the busted lip.

"Where is Derek?" I repeated slowly and full of menace.

He wiped his bleeding mouth with the back of his arm. He seemed surprised to see it when he looked down. I stepped closer, forcing him back against the fridge. The sour smell of cheap beer burned my nose. It sent me back in time, and despite my rage, a familiar pang of adolescent anxiety twisted my stomach.

"Fuck you." He spat blood at the ground near my feet.

In one swift step, I had my forearm pressed against his throat. He gasped and fought me but he was too drunk to cause any damage.

"Where is your son, you worthless piece of shit?"

He sputtered, his already ruddy face growing purple. I relaxed enough to let in breath.

"The bastard took his whore sister and left. They aren't my problem now. I don't fucking care."

My entire body screamed with the desire to press until he collapsed to the ground. He didn't even care about them. They were useless to him now as legal adults and he still hurt them. Anger burned up my body. Jack couldn't hurt this monster, not with his ties to Tiple F, but nothing said I couldn't take matters in my own hands. I leaned into his throat more.

He must have read the thoughts in my eyes and realized the seriousness of the situation.

He tried to speak again, so I loosened my grip.

"They sometimes go to their friend's place. The queer."

I closed my eyes and grit my teeth. I really did not want to go to jail for murder.

Or did I?

No.

I stepped back. He slumped back gasping.

"Fuck it." I stepped forward and punched him once in the eye, putting my entire body into it.

He cried out and fell back swearing me out. I shook my hand out, hiding my wince, because *fuck* that hurt.

"If you ever lay a finger on any one of those kids, I will break your fucking neck. Do you understand?" I had to speak slow or risk biting my lip. I was so shaken with rage it was bound to happen.

"You can't do this," he sputtered holding a hand to his eye. Impressively he still held the can of beer in his other hand. "I'm calling that fucking place and reporting you."

"I don't work for them. I'm a friend of your son's. You're a coward. You're a worthless piece of shit and you will never see these kids again. You think you're some big man because you take your own miserable pain out on children? You disgust me. The only thing that brings me peace is knowing that this pathetic existence is your life." I gestured to the house around me. The walls were stained and cracked. The whole place smelled stale and was months from being condemned. "You will rot away here and nobody will find you until your corpse smells so bad the neighbors complain. I hope rats feed on your putrid body." I spoke without stuttering or biting my lip. It was all the words I wished I had told my own father. Something inside me felt free. I shook head to toes with rage but had said exactly what I meant. "Maybe one day you'll understand the gifts you lost but I doubt it."

He stared up at me glaring. "I don't know who the fuck you—"

I jumped toward him and he scrambled back. Point made. "Coward," I spat.

I turned and left him swearing and moaning as I stomped back out of the house.

I might regret that later but now I couldn't care less. I had to find Derek and his sister. Ethan was the one who messaged me Derek was in trouble and I still had his address from when Ford had given me their info. But Ethan had been MIA since then. I hadn't wanted to involve Jack. I wanted to take care of this for him and leave Triple F completely out of it. But that was no longer an option. Especially since I might have criminal charges pressed against me. I needed his help to find Ethan and Derek and he probably needed to know that I punched Derek's dad in the face. Not that he would mind. Only that he should know.

I had just unlocked my phone to call him when Ethan finally texted me back. It was a dropped pin to a location and the words "found him." I put it in my map and immediately headed that way.

I got there in minutes. I double-checked the address to make sure it was right. I parked in the high school parking lot and another text popped up.

"Under the bleachers," Ethan's text read.

I ran to the football field and found them almost immediately. What was it about bleachers that made teens feel so safe?

Ethan, Derek, and the sister, I presumed was Chloe, stood huddled under the bleachers. Chloe shared their jet-black hair but hers was long and straight. She wore thick eyeliner and had dark slashes for eyebrows. She spotted me first and stepped behind Ethan. Derek shot a glance to her before noting my arrival.

"Brawny Man," Ethan said lightly.

That was my first indication something was going on. Derek gave me a sly grin.

"Are you hurt?" I asked him.

"Hurt?" He threw out his arms to show me. "I'm fine."

"But your dad ..." I had assumed that the split lip had come from some altercation. I looked to Ethan. "You said Derek was in trouble."

Ethan scratched at the back of his neck. "I said he needed you."

Chloe moved out from behind him. "Oh, this is him?" She tucked her hair back and smiled at me. "Hi, I'm Chloe." She held out a limp hand.

I shook it and looked to Ethan. "William." My head processed everything as fast as it could but nothing made sense. "Your dad looked busted up."

"My dad?" Derek asked confused. "When did you see him?"

"I just left his house." I felt less worried for them by the second but a different anxiety grew.

"We moved out last month. The second we were eighteen. Ethan's mom has been letting us crash on the couch until we find a place. As far as my dad ..." Derek frowned at the ground.

"He gets in fights at Dragon Bar all the time." Chloe tossed her hair over her shoulder.

"What's going on?" I said to Ethan.

"Look. I hadn't meant for you to go there." Ethan held up his arms like he was trying to calm an angry bear.

"Fuck," I swore under my breath, running a hand over my face. "I punched him in the face. He could press charges," I said.

Ethan laughed into his fist. "Oh shit, that's awesome. I wish I could have seen it."

Chloe and Derek shared a look I didn't like. Despite all the shit, they were still his kids. There was no accounting for what that bond made people feel.

"Ethan. If you don't tell me what's going on, I will lose my shit," I said gravely.

"Skip?" His deep voice sent chills down my spine.

I spun on my feet toward Jack. His eyebrows furrowed in concern, a phone in one hand. He was more gorgeous than I remembered. The whole world dimmed around him where he shone like a beacon in the night.

"Jack," I breathed his name.

He was a little disheveled, for him at least. His usually short-cropped hair grown out a little and his beard longer than I'd seen it. As he stepped closer, the bags under his eyes told me he'd been sleeping as well as I had been.

"What's going on?" He looked at each of us. "Are you okay?" he asked Derek.

"I'm fine." He turned to his friend. "Jesus, Ethan. I told you this was a stupid fucking plan," Derek said.

Jack stepped closer. "So I don't need to call the police? You aren't hurt?"

Derek shook his head. "Look. We just wanted you two to talk."

"You've both been fucking miserable for months," Ethan added to Jack.

It all clicked into place. Jack slid his phone into his pocket, his other hand pressed to his chest in relief.

I dropped my head down. "Shit."

"And I knew that Brawny Man was in town this week ..." Ethan trailed off.

"We've been played," I said to Jack.

Jack went perfectly still. His expression unreadable.

"And I might have caused some additional problems," I added.

"He punched that asshat in the face!" Ethan said excitedly.

Jack closed his eyes and took a deep breath.

"I didn't know about any of this," I explained. "I didn't mean to punch him ... I just—" I felt the shame of my actions start to creep in. What if I put Triple F in serious jeopardy?

Jack shook his head at the ground. "I'm just jealous I didn't see it." When he lifted his head, his dimples were full on.

All at once I felt like I could take a breath in for the first time in months. The look he gave me held so much I wished three teenagers weren't standing nearby.

"That's what I said!" Ethan said excitedly.

Jack held my gaze as hard as I held his.

"Oh okay, I see," Chloe said to Ethan.

"Told you. The heat, it burns," he replied in a dramatic voice.

"Why don't we let them talk. That was the whole point of this after all," Derek said.

Distantly I was aware that the three of them stepped away. I should be annoyed at their machinations but I couldn't be. Not with Jack here. Everything I had been feeling locked into place instantly. Whatever else didn't matter. Only he mattered.

Jack stepped forward. "I have wanted to call—"

I didn't let him finish. I grabbed the back of his head and waist, pulling him to me. I wrapped my arms around him so tight he probably couldn't move even if he wanted to. He stiffened and then relaxed as his own arms wrapped tight around me.

"God, I've missed you," I said as I held on for dear life.

"Skip," he said.

"I should have called. I don't know why I-I didn't." I closed my eyes tight as I inhaled his clean scent.

"Shh, it's okay. I know. Me too." His voice was tight as his hand smoothed up and down my back.

"I was so scared. You wouldn't believe," I said.

"Believe what?"

"There's only you. It's only ever been you. I had to get my head on straight but S-S … there's nobody else. It's just you."

He pulled back, cupping my cheek in his hand. "I was an idiot to push you away. I was scared too."

His mouth was on me. We kissed with all the desire the last few months had taken from us.

"I'm so sorry," I said between breaks.

"I love you." He kissed my nose. My cheek. My closed eyes.

"I love you too."

We had so much to say, so much to explain. But all we could do was hold each other. I couldn't stand another moment away from him. I'd wasted too much time already.

I grabbed his hand.

"Let's go to my house," he said.

"What about the kids?" I asked.

"We can deal with them later."

We walked back to the parking lot hand in hand.

It all felt so good. All the years of never being sure, all clicked into place. I would love him no matter what. We would figure everything else out. It didn't matter. I looked up at the stars. How could I have let myself waste any time where our lives were so short? A flicker in the grand scheme. I couldn't waste a moment more.

I turned to Jack, grateful for everything that led to that moment. He smiled at me in a way that told me he felt exactly the same.

I saw the headlights then. Moving too fast. Too erratically.

Time slowed in a way I'd never experienced.

A truck careened through the parking lot. A man with a black eye and split lip behind the wheel with disgusted rage in his eyes. Too fast. Coming right at us.

Jack.

Right there in the path of being hit. He was looking at me like I was everything. Completely unaware of the madman trying to take the most wonderful person from the planet from me.

There was no time to debate. I acted. I pushed Jack away as hard as I could. I braced myself for impact.

The flash of headlights. A loud snap. Shocking pain.

Blackness.

CHAPTER 16

SKIP

*T*he heavy steps of male boots woke me from my haze. For the first time in as long as I could remember, I was disappointed to see Sanders standing in front of me. Sanders looking pitiful, worried, and like a burned-out European soccer player.

I gripped my sheets and turned to the window, not ready to face him. "I'm going to be fine," I said. "You didn't have to come all the way down here."

"Come on, mate," he said in a choked voice.

I'd moved out. I'd tried so hard to move on. Sanders and I spoke a few times to wrap up the final clients of OTB but that was it. I'd hardly seen him since I was busy wrapping up a few clients and took several trips out to Green Valley to help Ford with Triple F. I was trying to show Jack that I was ready to live the life that I wanted. I was ready to show him that there was nobody else for me. Instead, I spent the last few months feeling more alone than ever. All the emotions came to the surface the moment I saw Sanders. How could I have ever thought I was in love with him? I loved him, of course, but there was nothing comparable to the potent devastation of having Jack and losing him.

"Of course, I'm here," he said.

I couldn't hide the anger on my face when I turned back to him. I didn't *want* to hide what I felt anymore. If Sanders and I wanted to move on in our friendship, I couldn't hold anything back anymore.

He pulled up the chair next to the bed and sat down. "I hate this. I hate everything I've done. I hate seeing you like this," he said.

His emotions were right there on the surface. He looked miserable. It softened me because I knew he was a mess too. We all were.

"Sucks, doesn't it?" I asked. "Seeing somebody you care about in a hospital bed?"

He held my gaze and nodded. We both knew we needed to hash this out once and for all.

"Imagine seeing it all the time. Imagine seeing the most important person to you in the world, constantly putting themselves in danger, making stupid choices and not giving a shit how it impacted those around them," I said.

"I know. I've been so selfish. I'm sorry. I've been talking to a therapist. I know I was putting myself at risk because I—I didn't want to go out like my father. And losing my mom so suddenly. I guess it messed with me in ways I didn't even recognize. But I never did it to hurt you."

"Yeah, but you did," I said harshly.

Maybe I wasn't being fair but these last few months were so hard on me and I needed a friend too.

"I'm so sorry."

"You didn't care," I said. "You never cared enough to call before you left. To say where you were going. But I was always there, wasn't I? Walking behind you, sweeping up the pieces all too eagerly. You let me." Jack had been right about that part at least. Maybe I wasn't in love with him like Jack thought, but we did hold each other back to stay in this comfortable bubble. To try to stay protected from getting hurt.

To Sanders' credit, he just listened. Didn't try to deny anything. It seemed he had changed as much as I had.

"We're done with this, Sanders," I said but couldn't quite meet his gaze.

"What?" His voice cracked and I felt it just above my heart.

"This enabling of each other."

"I'm sorry," he repeated.

Heat burned my ears and my vision blurred. I had to get this out. I needed to say this. "I deserve better," I said.

"Fuck yes, you do. I want you to be happy. You deserve everything."

I went on, "I needed you when Dad died. And you left." I needed to share with him about Jack and all the heartache and fear of our shared night together but I never felt like I could share that with him.

"I've been so selfish."

"I know you were in pain. I was hurting too," I said.

"I'm not gonna do it again, mate. I'll show you in a hundred ways. Whatever you need."

I sighed preparing to say the thing I had been fearing the most. The truth that I thought would damage our friendship irrevocably. This could be the reason Sanders kept me around. What if, after this, I never heard from him?

"I think it's time to close down OTB." The words tangled on my tongue and I started over. "No. I know that I don't want to do OTB anymore. It was always your passion and not mine."

"Okay." He nodded once, his face serious. "We will work out the details when you're better. There aren't any clients right now anyway."

I blinked at him. Okay. He was still here. I should have trusted in our friendship more. I shouldn't have doubted it but just having him stay and know I meant more than the business, meant everything. Jack had been right. Gretchen had been right. When you loved someone and cared about them, you wanted their happiness no matter what. Even if it didn't align with your own plans. Why had I doubted that Sanders would want that for me? Our whole lives together he had always strived to make me happy. When had I thought that changed?

I collected myself and asked, "You're talking to someone?"

"Yeah. They're helping me work through some shit."

"Good. You're allowed to be more than one thing, Sanders. I'm your best friend for who you are, not because you can charm a car salesman out of his coat." The words slipped out but I knew they would never stop being true.

He smiled a huge, real grin for the first time since he got here. A tear balanced on his eyelid. "I'm glad I haven't fucked it up so bad."

"You have a lot of making up to do. Not just to me." Roxy and I had talked a lot since he left. He owed her big-time.

"Oh yeah, I know," he said.

"Strength comes from living through the pain, not ignoring it. Your father told me that."

He reached for my hand and I squeezed it back. We shared a moment thinking of William.

"Skip!" Roxy's worried voice brought both of our attention to the doorway.

I glanced to Sanders to find him watching her wide-eyed and hopeful. These two really needed to talk.

* * *

Jack

I WALKED into the hospital room with shaking hands and a lump in my throat. I almost broke down when I spotted him in the bed, his foot in a cast.

"Skip?" I gasped.

I hadn't been able to go with him to the hospital. I had to take the kids back to my house, to keep them safe while we did all the police paperwork. Derek and Chloe's father was going away for a while and with the custody order he wouldn't be able to hurt them or anybody else for a long time.

This was my first time seeing Skip since he saved my life. He *saved* my life.

"Jack," he said. His lips were tight and his color was pale.

"Are you okay?" I walked toward Skip, desperate to reach for him but still so unsure about everything. I ended up keeping my hands in my pockets.

Skip scooted up higher in the bed and tucked some stray hairs back. He looked more gorgeous than I remembered, even battered.

He held my gaze, my intense stare making him blush.

"I feel ridiculous. It's just a broken bone. I'm going to be fine," he said.

I examined him from head to toe, feeling my eyes welling. He looked so fragile like this. I couldn't stand it. He was so big and strong; he shouldn't ever be hurt.

"We'll just go and see if we can find some coffee," a voice said.

Only then did I notice the other occupants of the room, Roxy and a haggard-looking Sanders. She was dragging him out but I couldn't care less. I only saw Skip. My Skip.

As soon as they were out of the room, I brushed hair back off his forehead. He had a deep scratch that had been cleaned and glued.

"I can't believe that you did that," I said, my voice tight. "You saved my life, Skip."

He swallowed and his Adam's apple bobbed. "You saved mine first," he said.

I gasped out a tight cough. I couldn't find the words. I couldn't believe we wasted any time when this was so real. How could I have ever denied it? I hadn't even cared when I saw Sanders sitting there. Sanders had nothing on what I felt for Skip.

He seemed to understand too. He nuzzled into my hand.

"How are the kids?" he asked.

My heart pounded. Whatever worries I had, whatever stupid petty fears that held me back were gone the moment I saw him again. When that truck hit him, my worst fears were realized. I could never lose this man. Whatever it took, we had to give us a try.

"They're fine. Shook up. At my house."

"And that asshole?"

"Jail. The kids are pressing charges. They're going to get a restraining order too if he manages to get bail."

Skip let out a sigh and leaned back.

"I didn't know you were back," I said. I wanted to finish our earlier conversation. Put the past behind us so we could move forward.

He turned toward me. "I didn't know what to say. I was trying to work through some stuff. I thought about calling you a hundred times."

"Me too." I swallowed. "I'm sorry for pushing you out that night. I just wish—"

"No. You were right to. I had to get my head on straight." He held my gaze.

"I'm sorry I didn't trust you. I was so afraid."

"I understood how it looked from where you are. Just know something. I've been doing a lot of thinking. I do love Sanders. I always will."

I stared at my thumb moving over the back of his hand. I couldn't let go. "But it is nothing like what I feel for you," he finished.

I looked up to him.

"I think … I thought that I owed him. I thought maybe he was the only person who knew me. I was so wrong. You've always known me. And I love you, Jack. I think I have from that very first night."

I smiled and felt my lip quivering. "I love you, too."

"Sanders is my best friend but that's all he will ever be. I had been making some changes in my life. I was here already because I was ready to tell you some things."

"Like what?" I smiled.

He scratched his chin. "I guess mostly all that." He gave me his half smile. "I just felt so damaged. So unsure of who I am. You seemed so … complete. So sure of who you are. I felt like I wasn't enough."

I snorted. "I have nothing figured out. Maybe I thought I did, but I was just as scared as you. I felt so much for you, so fucking fast. I was terrified. And then when I saw you with Sanders." I shrugged and felt embarrassment burn the back of my neck. "Just good old-fashioned jealousy."

"You have absolutely nothing to worry about. I promise." He looked deep in my eyes.

"I know. And there are things I need to work through too."

His face shuttered.

"But I was thinking. There's nothing that says we can't do that together?"

Tension melted from his shoulders. "Yeah?"

"Yeah," I said. "Who ever said people need to come together fully formed? The way I figure, we have years and years to figure out who we are and what we want. And even then we will grow and change."

"True." He smiled a full smile, slightly twisted, and there was that infamous heart skip.

"I think though, as long as we do all that together …"

"I agree. It just makes sense. Because being away from you has broken me." Skip pulled my hand up to kiss it.

"Me too. I've been miserable," I said.

"Let's not do that again."

"So what does that mean for us?"

"I'm not sure. Let's figure it out together?"

"Deal." I bent forward and kissed him gently on the lips.

He grabbed the back of my head and deepened it. When we broke apart, I kept my forehead pressed to his.

"I've missed you so fucking much," I panted.

He nodded against me.

At the moment, Sanders burst back into the room with a goofy grin on his face. I released Skip and stood back.

"Oh no," Skip said.

"What?" I looked to Skip and then his monitors.

"Sanders has crazy-idea eyes," Skip said.

"Oh boy, do I!" Sanders rubbed his hands like a maniac.

"Did you and Roxy figure things out?" Skip asked.

"Not even a little," he said bright and confusing.

"So you're not happy?" I asked, looking between the two of them.

"No. Not really. But I think I can be," he said. "But I'm going to need help."

I shared a knowing look with Skip. Whatever came next, we would figure it out together.

CHAPTER 17

SKIP

I went back to Jack's house the following day and stayed. My life in Denver was over. I hadn't discussed all the details with Jack yet, but I had already started the process of moving here. Sanders had big plans to woo Roxy that somehow involved tight pants. I was sure that they were going to work things out and that I would need to be here to help Sanders set up with the Lodge. Not because he needed me here but because I wanted to be here. We had a long talk and we both understood that we needed to explore a life that didn't revolve around the other but we were still best friends.

I would figure out what to do next.

"Here." Jack patted the pillow and helped me into the bed. "We will use the downstairs guest room until the cast is off."

"And you're sure you don't mind if I stay with you for a while?"

He gave me a look like I was a fool. He had just helped me shower and was now pampering me like I was helpless. I guess he did want me around.

"What about Suzie and Ford?" I asked.

"They'll be happy to move out on their own. They'd been staying here to help me out but I know they need their own space."

He flopped into the bed next to me. He looked me up and down in a way that made my cheeks flush.

"I have been thinking about that though," he said.

"Thinking about what?" I asked. I wanted to be official. I wanted to live with him. I needed to hear the words that it was just us now.

"I love this house. I've thought about you living here with me."

"It's a beautiful house," I said, my heart hammering with hope. "I've also thought about living with you here too."

"But I don't think that will work."

I frowned. "Okay."

"It's just a lot of house. And with your cast … I think it's time for somebody else. What if Ethan and the twins moved in?" he asked.

I blinked in surprise. "Really?"

His hands were clasped on his stomach and he looked at the ceiling. "I would rent it out to them. A trial period. I'll still own it just in case."

In case their love triangle blows up in their face? I thought but didn't say. For once being in my thirties felt like a gift. I wouldn't want to go back to that time.

"I think that's a great idea," I said. And I did. I was only a little disappointed.

"It's time for the next generation. After all, it was someone else taking a chance on me that got me here in the first place."

I shifted so that I faced him. "I trust Ethan. I think he'd do anything to prove himself to you."

"I'm happy to see him thriving. Derek and Chloe, too, already seem better just having moved out."

"This house is a huge upgrade from the couch," I said.

He nodded. "I think it will be good for them. Maybe being around the college will get them to think about it. The twins never thought that they had a future, I don't think they know what to do now."

"It will be good for them all," I said. My palms grew clammy. What about us? I just needed to ask. What about us?

"Gretchen knows a place that we might be able to rent in Green Valley. If that doesn't work, we can go anywhere. It might be better to be on the ground floor for a while anyway until you're done with your PT."

I laughed out a sigh of relief and snuggled into his arms.

He pulled back to look at me. "What?" he asked.

"Nothing. I think that sounds good."

"Okay, good. Because being apart is not an option." He gave me a knowing smile.

I kissed him.

"I want to make this work," I said.

"Me too." He shifted to face me.

His lips met mine and we kissed. And kissed. And kissed like we were making up for lost time. We rubbed together until we both panted with need. I shifted to get closer when my leg reminded me of my current predicament.

"I hate this cast," I ground out.

We had so much time to make up for. So much that I wanted to do with him.

"Me too." He sat up and pulled off his shirt. "But there are ways to work around it."

The mischievous glint in his eyes had me licking my lips. "Oh yeah?"

He helped me take off the boxers I had put on after the shower but thankfully wasn't wearing anything else. He stripped naked and I admired his beautiful physique.

"You know, I was promised a dance," I said, my gaze moving all over him.

He lowered his hand to his dick and stroked. "I don't think that would be safe right now." He moved some pillows to prop my leg up and to the side. His head lowered to kiss up my thighs before taking me into his mouth.

"Later is fine, I guess," I gasped out.

He continued to work me with his mouth as I thrust into him. "This feels unfair. You'll have to do all the work for a while."

I popped out of his mouth.

"Oh no," he said flatly before licking me from balls to tip. "Whatever will I do."

I smiled and beckoned him closer. "I need to taste you."

He walked on his knees until I was able to take him in my mouth. He groaned as I did my own finest work.

Then we spent many, many hours making up for lost time.

* * *

Jack

"COME ON, we're gonna be late!" I called down the hall toward the bedroom where Skip was still getting ready.

"Coming!" he yelled back.

I shifted by the door where Suzie and Ford waited with me. We all decided to meet at the house before taking one car to the Lodge. It was our last night here before Ethan, Derek, and Chloe moved in.

I paced in a circle and checked my watch one more time.

"Well, well. How the tables have turned," Ford said giving me a knowing laugh.

"Oh be nice. Look how nervous he is." Suzie came and straightened my bow tie.

"I'm not nervous," I said and my voice cracked. "Do I look okay?"

"You look very handsome," she said.

"Like a million bucks," Ford agreed.

I gave a weak smile before wiping my hands on my suit pants. I needed to calm down before I gave myself away. Triple F was having a banquet at the Lodge to thank the donors. Devlin and Kim were going to perform together and hopefully the draw would raise more money. But that wasn't what I was nervous about.

Footsteps creaked the wooden floor behind me.

I turned around and gasped a soft breath in.

Skip smiled nervously. "This okay?"

He wore a black suit, cut tight to his muscular frame. His hair was slicked back and held in place with product and his beard was trimmed short. His cast was off now and he walked without a cane.

Suzie let out a low whistle.

I collected myself and found my voice. "You look amazing."

We came together and I kissed him lightly on the cheek not wanting to mess up any of his perfection.

"You too," he said giving me a heated once-over.

I mean how important was this banquet anyway when we could stay here and spend the night taking off each other's clothes?

"Don't look at me like that, or we won't be leaving at all," he whispered in my ear. Louder he said, "We better get going."

I shook my head and smiled. My hands shook as we all made our way out to the car.

The drive went too fast. The speeches blurred by. I talked to people. I made conversation, I'm sure, but I couldn't remember any of it. I barely recognized the main lodge all decorated up. Roxy had outdone herself to make it look amazing but I couldn't focus on any of it. Devlin and Kim's performance was lost on me. Several times Skip lightly elbowed me to check that I was okay.

By the time many people moved to the dance floor, I couldn't take it anymore.

"Can we talk? Outside?" I asked Skip.

He shot me a worried look and nodded.

As we headed outside, we passed Gretchen talking to Vincent, that New York guy Roxy worked with. She spoke animatedly and he had his nostrils flared. I was vaguely aware that she was up to something again but couldn't focus on anything but my racing heart.

Once we were on the terrace, the cool winter night helped calm me down. I focused on the stars and thought of that first night I watched Skip under them. He looked at them like they were magical. I gathered the courage that image brought. I had planned this speech a hundred times, gone over it time and time again with Ford. I knew I had nothing to be worried about and yet ...

"Are you sure you're okay?" Skip asked, gently pressing a hand to my cheek.

"Um, umhumm." I scratched my neck and double-checked my pocket for the hundredth time.

"You seem to have shortness of breath," Skip said. He pressed two fingers to my neck. "Your heart is racing." I blinked at him. "Trouble speaking?"

I nodded.

"You're sweating too."

"I—"

"I would hate for you to have a panic attack right now. Not when I'm getting ready to propose to you," Skip said.

"No, it's not—"

I leaned back to look at him as his words hit me. He dropped slowly to his knees in front of me. He held a box in his hands and his sweet half smile. "Jack. Ever since I saw you, in between the finest drag queens in Tennessee, I knew you were meant to be in my life. The more I spent time with you, the more I discovered you were one of the kindest, sexiest people on this planet." He spoke so clearly, with confidence and not a single trip-up. But no. This wasn't how this was supposed to go.

"Wait. No!" I dropped to my knees.

"No?" He reeled back.

"No. Yes," I added quickly. "I mean yes, but no!" I pulled out a box that matched his own in size.

His eyes widened. He looked from me to the box and back to me. "I-I—"

I laughed. "I know."

"But I had a whole speech planned," he said, his eyes gleaming.

"Me too." I laughed and wiped away a tear.

"So then, is it a yes?" he asked.

"Only if you say so," I said.

We laughed and cried as we slid gold bands on each other's fingers with shaking hands.

A moment later a ruckus broke out behind us. Suzie and Ford, followed by Roxy, Sanders, Devlin, and Kim all poured out onto the terrace. Shortly after, Gretchen joined them smoothing her shirt and fixing her hair. As soon as she saw us both on our knees, she cackled with laughter.

"Oh it's too perfect!" she called out and snapped a picture.

The group laughed and congratulated us.

"Did you know?" I asked them shocked.

Suzie laughed with a nod. "I couldn't wait to see."

"Skippo told me," Sanders said.

"I may have let it slip to Suzie," Roxy added.

"Then at the last SWS meeting, we put it all together," Kim said sweetly.

She grabbed Devlin's hand and smiled at us.

"Got the whole thing on video." Suzie smiled.

"I thought you were about to pass out, Jack," Sanders said.

I smiled at him. "I was."

He threw an arm around my shoulders and grinning ear to ear. He gently pulled me to the side and whispered, "If you ever hurt him, they will never find your body." His smile was still in place and nobody would have been the wiser.

I held his eyes and said, "Ditto."

He threw back his head and laughed, shaking my shoulder. "You're a good egg, Jacko."

The rest of the night was a blur of champagne and laughter and tears.

Later that night I held Skip in bed, having just celebrated our new status as fiancés. I laughed and shook my head, remembering how crazy the proposal had gone. He kissed my forehead, seeming to know exactly what I was thinking.

"Think this will change anything for Triple F?" he asked.

"Nah," I said. "I think since you are already working there, it doesn't matter. I think the kids will be happy for us."

"Good," he said.

"I do think we should petition Ford for a name change though. Anything has to be better than Triple F."

"Well, now that it's getting so big, we may have to. It's not just Ford's kids anymore, is it?" Skip absentmindedly ran his hand up and down my back sending shivers over me. "They're so important to me now."

"It happens fast, doesn't it," I said.

"I feel … happy," he said. "I feel like I'm doing something with my life, you know?"

I nodded. "Hmm."

"I like helping at the Lodge and doing the corporate stuff sometimes too. But being with you and being here. It all feels right."

"It does. I'm glad you're happy. I'm happy too."

"Did you ever think, starting where we did, that we'd get here?" he asked, his throat tight.

"No. I never let myself dream so big. Not until I met you."

"You and me. It's like we were destined to meet."

I lifted up to smile at him. "Who knew you were so romantic."

He shrugged and blushed. I would never get tired of that blush. I would never get tired of this man. No matter what happened, how we grew and changed, I would do it by his side.

"I love you."

"I love you, Skip," I said and lowered my head back to his chest. Eventually, much later, I fell asleep to the steady sound of his heartbeat.

ACKNOWLEDGMENTS

Hello reader!

I hope you enjoyed Jack and Skip's love story as much as I enjoyed writing it. One of the most amazing and occasionally distracting parts of being a writer is when side characters demand a Happily Ever After of their own. Jack had been on my mind since *My Bare Lady*, just waiting for me to introduce the right person into his life. The moment he interacted with William/Skip I saw what was happening. I was so invested in these two that this story basically wrote itself as I wrote *The One That I Want*. I couldn't give Sanders and Roxy their own happy ending before I ensured these two got theirs—so to speak. ;) I am so grateful to Smartypants Romance for helping me get this out to you. While obviously not representational of all interracial relationships, I hope to have done justice for these two men and their beautiful love story.

Thank you also to the Sensitivity Reader who took the time to read my story and provide encouraging, helpful feedback.

Thank you to all the people who read and reviewed this early on. Brooke, Nicole, Tracy and Nora, you helped make their story stronger.

Thank you to my mom for showing me early on that love is love in all forms.

Thank you to my brother and his partner for showing how two nerds made their own lasting love story.

Thank you to my husband who unwittingly provides me with the best fodder for these books. (Also, all that unconditional love.)

Thank you to <u>Pipe's Peeps</u> for wanting to know more about all those long looks between Jack and Skip.

Every day I feel lucky that I get to share what love can look like in its many forms. And it's readers like you who make that happen. So THANK *YOU*!

ABOUT THE AUTHOR

Piper Sheldon writes Contemporary Romance and Paranormal Romance. Her books are a little funny, a lotta romantic, and with just a little twist of something more. She lives with her husband, toddler, and two needy dogs at home in the desert Southwest. She finds writing bios in the third person an extreme sport of awkwardness.

Sign Up for Piper's Newsletter!

Find Piper Sheldon online:
Facebook: http://bit.ly/2lAvr8A
Twitter: http://bit.ly/2kxkioK
Amazon: https://amzn.to/2kx2RVn
Instagram: http://bit.ly/2lxxV7H
Website: http://bit.ly/2kitH3H

Find Smartypants Romance online:
Website: www.smartypantsromance.com
Facebook: https://www.facebook.com/smartypantsromance
Twitter: @smartypantsrom
Instagram: @smartypantsromance
Newsletter: https://smartypantsromance.com/newsletter/

ALSO BY PIPER SHELDON

THE SCORNED WOMEN'S SOCIETY

My Bare Lady Book 1

The Treble With Men Book 2

The One That I Want Book 3

Hopelessly Devoted Book 3.5, A Scorned Women's Society Novella

THE UNSEEN SERIES

The Unseen Book 1

The Untouched Book 2

STAR CROSSED LOVERS

Midnight Clear - an introductory Novella

If the Fates Allow - coming Winter 2021

You can find all of Piper's books at pipersheldon.com

ALSO BY SMARTYPANTS ROMANCE

Green Valley Chronicles
The Love at First Sight Series
Baking Me Crazy by Karla Sorensen (#1)

Batter of Wits by Karla Sorensen (#2)

Steal My Magnolia by Karla Sorensen(#3)

Fighting For Love Series
Stud Muffin by Jiffy Kate (#1)

Beef Cake by Jiffy Kate (#2)

Eye Candy by Jiffy Kate (#3)

The Donner Bakery Series
No Whisk, No Reward by Ellie Kay (#1)

The Green Valley Library Series
Love in Due Time by L.B. Dunbar (#1)

Crime and Periodicals by Nora Everly (#2)

Prose Before Bros by Cathy Yardley (#3)

Shelf Awareness by Katie Ashley (#4)

Carpentry and Cocktails by Nora Everly (#5)

Love in Deed by L.B. Dunbar (#6)

Dewey Belong Together by Ann Whynot (#7)

Hotshot and Hospitality by Nora Everly (#8)

Love in a Pickle by L.B. Dunbar (#9)

Scorned Women's Society Series

My Bare Lady by Piper Sheldon (#1)

The Treble with Men by Piper Sheldon (#2)

The One That I Want by Piper Sheldon (#3)

Hopelessly Devoted by Piper Sheldon (#3.5)

Park Ranger Series

Happy Trail by Daisy Prescott (#1)

Stranger Ranger by Daisy Prescott (#2)

The Leffersbee Series

Been There Done That by Hope Ellis (#1)

Before and After You by Hope Ellis (#2)

The Higher Learning Series

Upsy Daisy by Chelsie Edwards (#1)

Green Valley Heroes Series

Forrest for the Trees by Kilby Blades

Seduction in the City

Cipher Security Series

Code of Conduct by April White (#1)

Code of Honor by April White (#2)

Code of Ethics by April White (#3)

Cipher Office Series

Weight Expectations by M.E. Carter (#1)

Sticking to the Script by Stella Weaver (#2)

Cutie and the Beast by M.E. Carter (#3)

Weights of Wrath by M.E. Carter (#4)